MW00995048

A MURDER COUNTRY

Kristen,
Wishing you the very
best. Enjoy the read...
B

PRAISE FOR
A MURDER COUNTRY

"In *A Murder Country*, author Brandon Daily has crafted a dark and beautifully written story of death and violence in a mystical landscape of tortured souls struggling with their innermost desires and demons. Daily's style is reminiscent of Cormac McCarthy at his finest, but with twists and turns that make this work uniquely his own. An excellent read!"

William Rawlings, author of *A Killing on Ring Jaw Bluff*

"Brandon Daily's mastery of language is simply staggering. I am in awe of his talent. This is the kind of book you have to put down every few pages and ask yourself did I really just read that? Can language really be that beautiful? But the pure poetry of the words is a seeming contradiction: Because what we have here is the most malignant depiction of humanity I've ever encountered. A humanity that can escape neither its own original sin, nor the brutal God who requires that man pay for that sin, in blood, throughout an endless cycle of pain. But it's not without hope. A sliver of it, anyway. Not without the promise of rebirth. The chance to try again.

You will hear this novel compared to the work of Cormac McCarthy. You're going to hear that a lot. And it's true, Daily is mining a dark American seam. He's of a tradition that starts with Hawthorne, and on to Poe, to Dickinson. From Melville, to Steinbeck, to O'Connor. And yes, to McCarthy. And now beyond.

You must read this book. But steel yourself."

Grant Jerkins, author of *A Very Simple Crime*

A MURDER COUNTRY

Brandon Daily

KNOX ROBINSON
PUBLISHING
London & New York

KNOX ROBINSON PUBLISHING

34 New House
67-68 Hatton Garden
London, EC1N 8JY
&
244 5th Avenue, Suite 1861
New York, New York 10001

First published in Great Britain and the United States in 2014 by Knox Robinson Publishing

A CIP catalogue record for this book is available from the British Library.

ISBN HC978-1-908483-67-6
ISBN PB 978-1-910282-20-5

Typeset in Trump Mediaeval

Printed in the United States of America and the United Kingdom.

www.knoxrobinsonpublishing.com

For Amanda,

and for my family

A MURDER COUNTRY

And the LORD God said, Behold, the man is become as one of us, to know good and evil: and now, lest he put forth his hand, and take also of the tree of life, and eat, and live for ever: Therefore the LORD God sent him forth from the garden of Eden, to till the ground from whence he was taken. So he drove out the man; and he placed at the east of the garden of Eden Cherubims, and a flaming sword which turned every way, to keep the way of the tree of life.

Genesis 3:22-24

1

A thin streak of light ruptures the black veil, throwing everything into a temporary clarity. A perceptible existence: one brilliant in contrast to the blinding darkness. Mountains form, trees and bushes and rivers are given shape, animals are constructed and the breath of animation is given unto them. And then, as quickly as the light appeared along the blackened horizon, it vanishes and the world is thrown once again into that voided darkness it had previously belonged, as if life itself is squandered away and plunged into the unknown abyss. And it remains so, forever awaiting that next flash to bring life once again to the land. A dry burst that may or may not ever come.

The storm had since passed. When The Rider looked up to the sky he could see no cloud nor trace that one had ever been. The sky was without a moon and only the blemishes of the stars spread across the vast darkness above him. Their glow gave only a hint of his presence as he crossed over from the edge of the wooded grove where the trees stood like druid guards in the night. He moved his way slowly, over the yellowing grass held captive by so many long days of summer, toward the small cabinhouse that waited like some darkening memory that time itself seems to be forgetting. All was darkness about the place, save for the obscure, hazy glow of candlelight that seeped from inside the house out, painting itself in dancing streaks and rays of hieroglyphic shapes on the ground through the glass windows that held the harsh world without from the quiet one within.

In the near distance, at the edge of the grove's reach, shaded by the trees and kept secret by the dark, a black horse stamped its feet heavily on the ground. Leaves crackled and twigs and chips of dry wood cried out under each powerful step, echoing throughout the night. The horse's breath showed in a misty fog. The silhouetted figure of The Rider stopped its stride and turned back to the trees, black against the bruising night-line, and let a low whistle escape his lips. Quiet followed: the horse waved its head from side to side, letting forth a loud spray from its nostrils before it tilted its head upward, peering through the labyrinths of branches and leaves and up towards the heavens.

A dog barked wildly from inside the house as The Rider made his way to the wooden steps leading to the door. On the other side of this door, the dog's paws scraped in uncomfortable streaks against the heavy wood, now stained and cracked from time and use. The shadow of The Rider stopped only yards from the steps. He waited in silence, still shrouded in darkness. He listened to the dog's crazed cries. Inside, the sound of a chair shuffled across the wood floor, then the door's latch being undone sounded in the quiet. The Rider could see the door open slightly and a large dog run out toward him at full speeded charge. Behind this animal, the gaunt figure of a man stood at the door and looked out briefly before shutting the door again.

Under his feet, The Rider could feel the dirt crumble and he shifted his weight to his back leg. The loose dirt surrounded his black leather boots, seemingly supporting them and locking them into the earth like some natural harness, keeping him.

As the dog chased toward the man, the latter reached slowly to his right side, drawing back the sweeping, heavy fabric of his black coat. From a leather scabbard he pulled a knife. Slowly, with precise and unhurried movements, the man rotated the blade in his hand, tightening his grip as he watched the dog draw closer at full run, it barking and baring its teeth, the white enamel glaring in the darkness—skeletons standing against one another in the dark of night. The reflection of the stars' glow shimmered against the heavy blade. He braced himself against the weight of the oncoming force. And then, when the dog jumped up at him, The Rider plunged the blade deep into the neck of the animal, and, with a quick sideways swipe, pulled the knife free of the fur and skin, feeling the stubborn rip of the tendons and muscle. The dog cried out in a sharp scream. And then quiet. At The Rider's feet it lay: its head curled back nearly resting on its shoulders; blood began to collect in a crimson black halo around its skull, trickling in the dust towards its paws and out farther toward the grove held just out of reach. He slowly wiped the bloodied knife on his pant leg, replaced it in its sheath at his side, and continued on to the steps.

Inside the rotting place sat an old man in a wooden rocking chair. He quietly swayed back and forth, his fingers drumming on his leg, keeping timed step to some distant melody playing along the shores of an untouched land. In this man's lap lay a black-bound Bible and he read attentively, following along with his fingers; he would occasionally lift his hand up from the page and smooth away the foggy, nonexistent demons from his eyelids.

Across from where this man sat, next to a dirty black stove furnace, was another rocking chair, and it too moved back and forth, this one creaking with every forward pull. In it sat a woman with dark brown hair wrapped and held up in a loose bun behind her head; some strands had fallen away from the rest and seemed to cling to the side of her sweatbeaded face. This woman was not as old as the man across from her, but she looked to be of similar age, maybe even older. Her dress was brown and white and touched the wooden floor even while she sat. At her feet lay a large goldyellow dog; its ears lay flopped on the sides of its head, its eyes closed, tongue stuck out through its shut mouth. The woman's hands worked fervently with yarn and needles and she would stop time to time and count the different rows she had already completed. Her eyes wandered about the house: to the table with plates of scrapmeat and cups of water still on it from supper. She looked to the dog at her feet and then to the left where the fire of the stove was still red and hazy within the opening—a mirage trapped within the dark prison. She then looked at the window to her right and then finally across to her husband who still sat reading, passing his fingers along the text, his mouth silently whispering the alien words to a deaf world.

"Yeh think he's aright out there?"

The man across the room looked up at her and then returned his gaze to the scriptured book on his lap.

She rested the yarn string down on hers. "Do yeh?" She squinted at him, trying to see the figure of her husband better. "Eli?"

He looked up again, this time shutting the book and placing it with careful precision on the floor next to the chair's rocking legs. He ran his fingers over his balding head, feeling the gentle pull of what hair there was still and the smoothed connection of his hands on his scalp. "He's all right."

"He's only a boy, though. Why couldn't yeh've gone out there with him like yeh usually do? Specially after that boy the other day. What if there's more of them thieves out there."

"He's old enough, Josiah is," the man muttered in response. "Needs to learn to fend fer himself like any other boy his age. Only a boy to yeh cuz he ain't been shown the world none." He tapped his heels against the floor, swaying the chair back and forth at a quicker beat. "Ain't my doin, neither. Yers."

"Yeh shoulda gone with him, Eli. He's still too young." Her eyes held an expression of fear and sincerity, of love and regret.

"When's he ever gonna be old enough to grow and live? Fer you that day ain't never comin to be. He can handle hisself out there. He's got guns. He don't need nothin else. Trust you me on that point. Boy's a good enough shot as any man I've known with it."

"I don't care. Still too innocent for that world out there. I seen it. You ain't seen it like me."

The man sighed. "The boy ain't even in the world out there. Off in the woods, surrounded. That's his protection. He don't need nothin else. God protects his own. Remember that."

The two sat for a moment, each looking at the other. Reflecting on life: the debts of living and costs of dying. Quiet now. After some time, the crackling embers in the stove sparked and sounded loudly in the room. Outside came a faint whistling sound that seemed to disappear even before it began; the sound was barely perceptible over the hiss of the furnace and the steady murmur of their breaths in the warmth of the room.

At the woman's feet the dog lifted its head quickly, its ears pinning themselves up, its nose twitching itself from side to side. Deep inside its body came a graveled rumbling that soon escaped from its throat. It lifted itself to its feet and ran to the door, panting and whining, its nailed paws screeching in clip-clopped step over the wood floor. The dog scratched hard at the door. The man watched the dog silently and after some time he pushed his chair back, letting the wood of the chair fight itself against the flooring, waking the quiet of its tender sleep, and he walked to the door. "Shut yer cryin," he murmured. Then he undid the latch of the door and let the yellow dog run out into the emptiness of the night. He looked out quickly and then shut the door behind him, hearing the click of the latch and the bark of the dog's calls in the world outside.

"Someone out there? Another thief, Eli?" The woman began to rise from her seat but sat back down, returning to her earlier stone-carved posture. She took up the yarn again and began to work it without thought. The needles clicked. She set it down again and looked at the man. "Is Josiah back? Is he, Eli?"

The man began to cross the room back to his chair. "Didn't see him. Damn mutt," he said. "Just loud and trouble." He was within arm's length of the chair when they heard the sharp yelp of the dog; the sound sliced through the space like a torrent of pain through a body and then all was quiet again except for the crackling of the wood in the stove and the sound of needles falling to the ground.

The woman started up and then sat back down. She looked at

the man.

"Stay here." He walked to the door, reaching out to his right and grabbing hold of the shotgun that lay perched against the wall. The steel was cold. His hands were warm from the fire across the room. His wife had stood and was inched close behind him. He opened the door quickly, pushing it out into the dark and he raised the shotgun to his shoulder and leveled it, pointing the barrel out into the abyss beyond the porch.

He could see the shadowed figure of The Rider slowly climb the steps to the door at a slow, deliberate pace. The steady sound of the heavy boot was offset by the cry of the spur, the metal shifting against itself, gently rapping on the wood below it with each step. The Rider's head was leaned down and he was watching his own feet shuffle upon each stair, studying their progression. His hat was black and low, curled slightly up at the sides and he wore a long black coat and pants; his boots tall and dark and heavy. The Rider's body seemed to escape into the dark of the night, becoming lost in the black trees and dead grass behind him. The old man moved back as The Rider reached the top step. "You lost, boy?" the man asked. His arms shook under the weight of the heavy gun.

The Rider slowly raised his gaze from his feet, bringing his eyes equal to the gun's barrel. In the flickering light from inside, the older man was able to decipher the other's form: he could see The Rider's face: the dark trimmed beard that covered the entirety of it, singular streaks of gray hiding themselves within the smooth patches, green eyes that shown yellow in the light, and a long red scar stretching itself from above The Rider's left eye and circling itself around and down midway on his cheek.

"You Eli Fuller?" The Rider asked. His voice was deep, gruff yet pleasing at the same time, a hint of a drawl from some unplaced region of the south. In it, there was a calmness. Behind him a dusty breeze was blowing through the woods, navigating the dark bases of the trees, rattling in the hollows and caves yet undiscovered.

"Can I help yeh with somethin?" He tightened his grip on the gun, his finger brushing against the trigger. Sweat began to form on his palm. His breath had become short. "Yeh seen my dog out there?"

The Rider stomped his boots on the outside porch. He looked down and saw the dirt and mud pieces that had fallen off and he scraped the pieces into a small pile with the toe of his boot and then he looked up. "You him?" He scratched at his face. "You Fuller?"

"Yeah," Fuller replied quietly, almost without words. His head nodded slightly.

"Then yessir, I believe you can help me." The Rider reached out and grabbed the shotgun that had been pointing at his face, directing the barrel away from him and then, with a quick flicker of movement to his side, The Rider pulled out from under his coat a revolver and shot. The sound crackled loudly and then it was lost in the oncoming silence. Fuller dropped the shotgun and fell hard to the floor. The Rider stood still, peaceably holding the revolver in his right hand, smoke still escaping from the barrel, the metal shining in the dull light. He stepped into the room, kicking the shotgun farther outside onto the porch with a shuffling sound and then he shut the door behind him. He stepped over Fuller, who was writhing in pain and clutching his leg. Blood was beginning to trickle from his clenched hands and was spreading out onto the floor. The Rider moved toward the woman, her hands trembling, spittle escaping her mouth in her panicked gasps. He reached out and held onto her chin and studied her face. Her eyes were red from tears, her features blank.

The Rider directed her down to the floor gently. She balanced herself on her knees. Shaking. A low cry escaped her lips. And then she slumped back and sat resting against the dirty wooden wall.

The Rider turned to Fuller. "Move over here," he said, motioning with his gun to where the woman sat. The man on the floor continued to hold his leg, his breathing becoming shorter and quicker than before. "Slide over here before I shoot you in the other one too." He leveled the pistol at the woman. She moved back farther against the wall, letting several sobbing gasps escape from her mouth. "I know you can move, Fuller."

Fuller turned his body on the ground so as to look at the man standing over his wife. She had lowered her head now and her face was buried within her arms. Her eyes were closed in the muted glow of the room. Above her, The Rider still stood. He continued to point the gun at her head. Fuller reached out with his hands and slid himself across the floor, leaving a bloody trail behind him—an abrupt swash of paint on an empty brown canvas. The Rider lifted the gun and held it up to his face, as if seeing it for the first time, examining some new found treasure in the light. Fuller sided next to his wife and pulled her body against his, cradling her tightly, as you would a newborn.

Josiah Fuller stepped carefully over the small running creek, balancing himself on rocks scattered just above the water's reach, watching his feet—their carefully placed stride. Water lapped around each of the stones, still perceptible in the moonless night's gaze. The streaks of light had moved off to the south and the west and all that was left now under the hanging branches of the trees was darkness. The steady trickling hum of the creek settled about him in a welcoming calm. In the distance, within the black gnarled fingers of the trees, stood a doe. Innocent and calm. Quiet. Its eyes seemed to reflect off of some spectral light. Its white speckled hide expanded and returned slowly to where it began as the animal drank from the cold rushing water, upstream from where the boy stood. The animal's ears twitched from the spraying mist of the creek. The boy stood, blending himself in with the trunks that lay scattered around him, becoming part of the natural world from which man had become set apart.

The shadows of the woods seemed to surround him in a welcoming grasp, holding him for the few venerable seconds with which he stayed immobile, haunting the evening with his piercing gaze upon the animal's purity, and in that fleeting moment he became the world as it was meant to be, as it was created. He raised the rifle quietly, feeling the tightness of the lever that held the bullet in its suspension; he took aim and breathed in and let the air out slowly. Then he pulled the trigger, caressing the cold steel with his finger, warm with the blood surging through his body, the blood that beaded the sweat on his back and loosened his legs of their tightness. The sound erupted through the trees, echoing in the deafness of the woods, dying out slowly into the peaceful void that had existed before he arrived. He watched the doe fall in silence to the water, graceful and without struggle. Through all this, the stream continued on its course, slowly, peacefully, beckoning out to an unhearing and listless world that had forgotten its name, its voice, and its touch until it had become simply another obstacle along the way.

The Rider drew back his long coat and holstered the revolver. He squatted down on his heels, dropping eye level to the two figures cowering on the floor before him; they had become merely façades of humans, outlines of people. He reached up and pulled the brim of his hat down, as if shading his face from the light of the room, hiding his face from some demon there behind him. His eyes were calm, a sad smile slowly fleshing itself across his face. "Ma'am," he said, tipping the brim of his hat at her.

He stood and walked toward the stove and took off his hat, revealing black hair smoothed back from his forehead. He knelt before the open stove. The embers were beginning to cool, the red turning to a muted orange, a light ocher color now within the darkening surrounds, growing fainter with each passing second. The wood inside was charred and black. He bent sideways, staring down some incubus arising from the vanishing inferno, some demon from the coals, letting the phantom of the sweltering heat caress his face, the sweat beads evaporating quietly and beginning anew in succession, dying even before their creation. He spat into the stove furnace and a hissing sounded, a spark of life in the desolation of the coals and wood, for what is fire but the creation of something from the utter and complete destruction and consumption of something else. He stood and looked back to the two huddled against the wall. He walked over to the rocking chair across from the stove, his heels clicking over the wood floor, scuffs ringing through the silent house.

The Rider sat in the old man's chair and let his feet shove his weight back; the chair returned the weight forward in mirrored manner, then back again. He kept swaying back and forth. "Thing bout chairs. Never can find a good one, can you?" He rested his hands gently on the arm rests, his fingers tapping in steady communicate to the naturalness of the wood—the unbreakable bond between the inner emotions of man and the earth from which he was formed, a bond easily forgotten: existence buried beneath the pressures of a maturing society, forgotten and removed from its own womb.

Fuller watched The Rider lull himself into a respite. The Rider's eyes wandered about the room, to the corners and even beyond, and in his eyes was a look of sadness and regret, as if he felt he were truly at home and at peace.

The old man looked at his leg and ripped the torn fabric of the pant free. The inner portion of his thigh had been torn off, the bullet having grazed the leg. Blood was beginning to dry along the flaked edges while more still raced in steady flow from the wound. He worked at tearing strips from the pant leg, wrapping them around the carved area and pulling tight. Tears flowed down his cheeks. His hands shook. Next to him, his wife had stopped crying and simply rested with her head hanging down, her hands covering her ears, blocking out the nonexistent sound.

The Rider broke himself finally from his trance and watched with fixed attention as the old man worked on his wound, then he looked above him. The sturdy ceiling overhead, some splinters in the wood covering. Fuller would need to patch those splits before the rain came, The Rider thought. The floor. The Rider looked at his own feet and his eyes caught hold of the black book at the side of the chair. He bent and picked it up and opened it to a random page. "You a holy man?"

Fuller looked up from tending his leg.

The other man didn't lift his eyes from the book. "This here." He held up the book. "You believe these here words?" The Rider looked up at Fuller and the woman. "You know them well?"

"God don't look after those like you. The damned burn in hell. I know that much."

"Depends." He settled back further in the chair. "Depends on who you ask. Depends on how you read this." He held up the book. "Depends on your god."

Fuller was silent. He wrapped his arms around his wife again, pulling her closer.

The stranger stood, his hand still clutching the book. With his other hand he pulled out his revolver again, looking at both outstretched in his hands, weighing their importance against each other. "Both these make men tell the truth, Fuller. In time they do. You see this. Both em. But, you put them together, then . . . then you can make even God say what's in his heart." He walked over to the two and stood before them. He didn't move. His coat surrounded him, embracing him in some unholy christening of darkness. "Lot of people sayin the world's gonna come crashin down. Gonna end soon they say. Apocalypse and burnin. Fire and death. Eleven years til the new time come. Nineteen hundred. Seems a long time, but it ain't really. I think that's what scares em. You one of them that think that way? Fuller?"

Fuller looked up at The Rider. His eyes lingering on the other's grip, relaxed and loose around the gun, tighter around the book.

The Rider knelt down, resting one knee on the floor. "No. You're probably one of them sensible ones right. You look out there," he nodded with his head, motioning out toward and past the door. "You look out there and you see that the apocalypse ain't comin. No, Fuller. It ain't comin." He shook his head. "It's already here. We're all livin it now. All of us. Been apocalypse since the reportin of time. The fire's burnin, sea's dryin, sky's paintin itself red. Right before our eyes, Fuller. All that's been happenin. Death, it's a way of life now. If you ain't shootin someone in the back then you better be watchin your own." He paused and looked thoughtfully to the book and then set it down carefully at Fuller's feet. He replaced the gun to his side.

Fuller looked at the book. A new surge of pain sped through his body and he grimaced.

"Let me tell you a story," The Rider said. He reached out and directed Fuller's face so that it looked directly into his own. "Ma'am," The Rider said quietly and patted the woman gently on her leg, "I want you to hear this story too." She looked up at him, her eyes wet and bloodshot. Her body continued to shake as from a spasm and her lip quivered as spit ran from the sides of her mouth.

"Story begins not too long ago, bout a week back. I was in the town out there, you know the one, not too far away. Bout seven or eight miles, I figure. Right? Anyways, I was just there passin through, grabbin a meal and a warm bed—the little luxuries of a life—and as I was ridin my horse out, I seen this mule drivin in a big wood trailer-sled. I figure it was full of some vegetables and whatnot, but then as I get closer to it I start to smell the rot of whatever it was bein carried in the back of that sled there." The Rider stood and walked about the room quietly. His hand brushed up against the revolver on his belt. He continued: "So I go up to the driver of that mule and ask him what he got stowed back there because all I could see was a big brown and yellow sacksheet drawn across the back, now mind you. And I could tell that somethin was there below it, but I wasn't sure.

"So, this man, nice little old man, long white beard—you probably know him, don't you?—anyhow, he stops the mule and shakes his head slow-like from side to side and then he turned in his seat on up there and he lifted up that sheet and I walked my horse on over a little closer til I was able to look down on whatever thing it might be that was hidden from sight. And now mind you, Fuller," The Rider turned back to Fuller, "that thing stunk like somethin I ain't never smelled, so much so that I didn't want to draw no nearer, but that is curiosity and so I went. And there below that sheet was the rottin body of this here boy." The Rider stopped and looked down at the ground, as if recalling the lost image back to his sight. His voice cracked a little as he talked. "And I wouldn't have paid it no mind really if it hadn't been for the boy's face, or what was his face where it should have been. All I saw was a big cave of where his eyes and his nose and mouth should have been. I seen just about half of that boy's right ear and then the rest was just carved in, like a rockcliff or somethin.

"And I grabbed the sheet from the man and lifted it higher—he didn't seem to mind me takin the sheet none—and that's when I saw the rest of the boy's body and I saw that he wasn't just shot in the head, but that he was shot at least twice in his chest too. Like as if whoever it was that shot him hit this boy in the chest once or twice and then went on at a closer pace and took to that boy's head. Aggression and anger behind it. Sin is what I saw when I looked at that boy.

"So I ask the driver what happened and he gave me your name. Says that you caught this boy there tryin to thieve you out of a horse—no means a innocent boy, I understand that—but that you caught him and went at him, makin him pay for whatever choice he done made. Now, I ain't sayin that the boy was right. In fact, he deserved what he got, but not by the hands of some farmer or mine worker none, not by someone like you, Fuller. But he told me all bout you and where I could find you out. And here I am."

The Rider walked over to the door and slowly opened it and looked out into the night, looking down the side of the house. To his right he could see the overhang of a roof that connected to the side of the house and below the roof was a wooden post that was dug into the ground. The Rider shut the door and then turned and looked at Fuller.

"Gotta ask you one thing, Fuller. Where's the horse that boy was tryin to thieve you of? I see your little stable on out there, but where's the horse?"

Fuller looked up. His eyes narrowed slightly. "Run off."

"Run off?"

"Two days back."

The Rider looked down at Fuller, judging the man's face, his breath and his eyes. Then he turned from the two and walked deeper into the small room. He shook his head. "All that trouble back there with that boy was all for naught, huh? Run off. Ain't that how it goes?" The Rider shook his head again.

The Rider walked over to the two and stopped so that his shadow covered them in dark. "I reckon that gun you killed that boy with is the same one you pointed at me, right?"

Fuller was silent. The Rider kicked Fuller's leg, making the man cry out in pain. "Right?" The Rider asked again. And Fuller nodded.

"Now, then, the true sin of this all is that that gun out there holds two shots. That means you shoot the kid and then you shoot him again. And judgin by the holes in that boy's chest he was done in. But then you load it again with two more shells . . ." The Rider pulled his revolver from his side and held it out just above Fuller's head. "And you snap it shut and you stand over that dead or dyin boy . . ." The Rider pulled the hammer of his revolver back so that it clicked loudly in the room. "And you get real close to him, maybe your gun is touchin his face even, and you pull the trigger again." The Rider fired, missing Fuller's head by a foot or so. The sound exploded in the room. The man and woman both drew further back against the wall, further back into themselves. In their ears all they could hear was a steady ringing that seemed to block everything else out. The woman put her palms against the sides of her head even harder. "And then you fired again." The Rider shot again, this time missing Fuller's head by only a few inches. Splinters from the wall flew off and scraped against Fuller's face, drawing some blood that began to run down his cheeks. "And you stand above that thing, because it ain't no human no more, and you watch as the blood and dirt mix and you may even think to yourself that you saved somethin, defended somethin, did somethin right. And that's how you justify it to yourself." The Rider walked back to the stove again. "But let me tell you somethin, Fuller, it wasn't your job to seek vengeance or retribution or punishment. Wasn't your job none. And that was your sin, and that's why I'm here today. To collect on that sin of yours."

Fuller looked down to his leg and then to the door. In his eyes he could feel the moisture beginning to form again. Truly feeling a sense of hopelessness for the first time. Regret and fear, knowing that he would forever forget the feeling of walking in the sun's heat. And he looked back to The Rider.

"That's apocalypse there. If you got no reservations bout shootin a kid, then I suppose life don't matter much anymore. It don't matter much," his voice seemed to trail off. "One minute a person's here, next not. One minute a kid runnin through the trees and tastin the cold of water and the next just a body heaped in some cart. Flies buzzin all around, bugs buryin themselves in your rot. Dirty. Body startin to smell. That's life. And the apocalypse is that life. It's already here." He gazed about the room, toward the door, then brought his eyes back to Fuller.

Fuller looked down at his wife next to him. Her body trembled, her arms feeling cold to the touch.

The Rider lifted the revolver and placed the barrel of it under the woman's tucked chin and raised her head higher. Her eyes were red but no longer wet. Her lip still quivering, her hands still blocking out the noise of the room. "Don't be doin that."

Fuller reached out and pushed the gun away from her face and brought her closer to him, her body almost resting on top of his. "She ain't done nothin. Let her go." His face was draining of color. His leg continued to bleed through the cloth.

The Rider shook his head, his face showing a pained expression. "I can't do that. Not supposed to." He took a deep breath and then let it out slowly. "She might not have done somethin directly," The Rider said, looking back to the woman, "but you were still here. You took part in this all, whether you realize it or not. You didn't stop him, and that was your decision that you made. And I'm sorry for that. I truly am."

He took off his hat and rested it on the floor. His face shimmered from sweat. There were thin gray streaks coursing the length of his long, matted hair. He looked back to Fuller. "You ain't answered me yet. You ain't told me if you believe these words. It's an important question." The Rider paused, waiting for a response, which he didn't get. He continued: "You just read them, or do you believe they're truth? God's own words, right?" He picked up the book again and thumbed through the pages with the barrel of the gun, holding the words of the scripture hostage. "Me, I suppose I look at God and the devil bit differently than most. They're one and the same, I believe."

Fuller looked off in the distance of the room; he let a hushed breath escape his parted lips. In that moment, he wished nothing more than to bathe himself in the icy waters of the river within the woods.

A smile played itself across The Rider's face, dancing as harmlessly as lightning bugs in a summer night. "I'm no preacher none, but I am different than you. There's God the father, then Jesus the son, who are both pretty near the same thing—same entity I once heard a man say. But then you got the holy spirit. Now, ain't nobody I talk to ever told me exactly what that is. A feelin they all say. No, that ain't it. This here holy spirit is Satan himself. The devil. You see now. Makes some sense if you think about it. They're all one. Linked and together. Continuin on forever. Without one, you can't have the other. That explains the good and bad in the world; that explains a lot. Don't you think?"

Fuller's eyes looked distant and they returned to The Rider, not looking at the man but through him. "True evil in the world. What's that then? That ain't God?"

The Rider smiled and then raised his hand to his forehead and with the back of his palm drew away sweat droplets that had begun to form. The shadows from the stove fire behind him licked at his face, throwing his eyes into a conspicuous darkness that lingered eternal. "Hot in here, ain't it?" He looked back to the stove. "Wood's almost burned through, though."

The Rider stood and walked over to the furnace and put two dried limbs of wood in the black gaping mouth, showering the stove's innards with sparks and ocher flames—flashes of a desert landscape at noon just as the sun scrapes the sand. The Rider walked back and kneeled down on the hard floor, his eyes becoming hazy in the growing heat, his hair sneaking its way onto his forehead, the sweat grabbing hold and baptizing it in the musky warmth of the room.

The woman looked up quickly and then down again, burrowing her face deep within the folds of her husband's shirt sleeve.

The Rider stood and walked back to them. He looked at Fuller. "I'm a different kind. One as old as this book." He handed the Bible to Fuller; the man took it and held it tightly to his chest. "Don't doubt your faith. All I can tell you now." His voice had dropped to a whisper, and there was a sincere, almost begging look on his face.

Fuller remained quiet.

"I seen many a people in your position, just like it is now, and I seen them think back on all they knew and all they believed before. It's important, though. Don't doubt it. One thing you can control is belief." He let a low sigh escape. "You read the old books much?"

Fuller stared forward, clutching the book tightly in his hands. The pain in his leg began to subside, numbness spreading through his body.

"Genesis is my favorite. Most people nowadays seem to bypass the old altogether, go straight for the new books. They want to forget about God's wrath—his jealous hate—look only at his love. Comfort themselves with Jesus. Makes them feel better bout themselves, I suppose. Makes them forget about their sinful lives, I say. You best hold that tight," he said, nodding to the book in Fuller's hands. With his left hand, The Rider pushed aside his coat and, feeling around in the darkness of his person, pulled from his pocket a small wooden tinderbox no bigger than a shotgun shell. He knelt down and laid the box gently on the floor.

The Rider's eyes were focused on the box as he meticulously worked his fingers, sliding one piece of wood from another so that there now were two pieces of wood on the ground: one a hollow shell and the other a box removed of a top that was complete save for the missing of the one side; in it were wooden matches stacked upon one another, the red heads lined in a row. He glanced up at the two, who still did not move, who still sat cradling each other. Blood continued to soak through the pant leg of the man and onto the floor, marking its territory on the ground below him and on the dress of the woman beside him. The streaks of blood on the ground from when Fuller had slid over earlier had turned black in the hazy glow of the room.

The Rider removed one of the matches from the box and looked at it, holding it in the air in front of his eyes. He waved it back and forth slowly, following it; he saw Fuller's eyes following in suit. The woman had raised her head and was now looking at her husband, her hands resting gently on his bloody leg. The warm liquid covered her hands, her breath shortening as the blood continued to pass from the cloth of the pant and collect in a pool below the tourniquet at his thigh.

"Strangest thing," the intruder whispered, thoughtfully. "Create fire at your fingertips. Power of God right here." He struck the match head against the wood flooring next to the box and light burst from the match; a crackling sounded, coughing and choking some before the blaze took complete hold of the match. Blue and green shades danced with each other at the center of the red and yellow. Nature's own mythical wonder. He held the fire close to his face. And, for the first time, his face could be fully discovered by the two sitting before him. The deep marks in his skin, the black hair about his chin and mouth, the deep red of his lips and pale turquoised green of his eyes like some remote lake surviving untouched in a child's fantasy. A narrow nose, red and raw from sun. The scar.

The Rider brought the gun's barrel up to his face, stroking his skin from his forehead down his left cheek, circling around his eye and down past his chin, flicking the end of the cold metal from his face, then bringing the gun up again and doing the same thing. "You see this here?" he said, motioning to the long scar—a streak where the skin raised in a pale pink. "Take a good note. Remember this mark." He took the gun and tapped it gently against his cheek. "This mark answers your question. It explains why I'm here, the way I am. Nature. I was created, just as you were, to be as I am. You can't change that. Creatin order in a world of unorder." He blew the flame out, throwing the space between them back to darkness. The slight flicker from the stove's light remained the room's only illumination. He replaced the gun at his side.

"My favorite story in that Bible there is Cain and Abel. Used to read it over and over when I was smaller, before this here mark was put on my face. It was the first murder. And I read it over and over, tryin to understand the reasons for God's unholy actions; used to wonder why God, all knowin, all carin—the same God who destined everybody's actions before they're born—why he would let that happen. Murder, hate. Never made much sense. And I'd ask myself whether my God was a lovin one, or a hatin one.

"But then I realized how death, it's all about order. Order in life. God and the devil are one. Two sides of the same stone. Neither one's true love, really, and neither's death or evil. They both are, switchin themselves til the only thing that makes sense is that there's no real sense to make of it all. Not in this world. Maybe not in the next neither. No sense at all. And it has taken me a very long time to accept that all myself."

The Rider stood and walked to the door, his spurred heels knocking against the wood floor. He opened the door and looked out onto the darkness encompassing his world—a world he felt he neither belonged nor one he could fully understand. "Still hot out there. Don't feel much like autumn, does it? Suppose it's still early. Snows won't be comin for a while yet, I reckon." He closed the door.

"I come to realize when I was younger that I am somethin more," The Rider said, turning. "More than you. Different, at least. I am God's angel in the flesh. I have been sent to search through the filth and mange of this world. And this scar is my Cain's mark. It's my purpose to report the souls of the wicked and lives of the oppressed to their judgment. I am Gabriel and Judas both."

He looked at his hands and then walked to the stove and picked up a loose log lying on the floor and set it in the smoldering flames, allowing the wood to begin to grow red and then charcoal and burn black. He removed the log and flung the flaming wood on the floor next to the rocking chair, across from where he stood and he walked over and reached down and picked up the yarn from the foot of the chair and placed it upon the burning log.

The flames rose and whipped around in such a sequential manner that it seemed controlled by some alkaline deity of despair and destruction far removed from the captive strains of time and of the earth. The flames rose, then dissipated some, and then rose again. Flaked pieces, ashen and spent, floated up and swirled about, dancing in the mid-air of the house before moving off into some uninhabited corner of existence. The chair began to redden with the near heat and then flames burst forth from the wood. A spreading pandemic moving about, each part of the house becoming afflicted by the pestilence. Raw beneath its own protected exterior, discharged and deranged on the inside, flooding to its surface, the phantom limbs of spirit leading forth and breaking through the bond of captivity, igniting first and then dying—rebirthing from the grave.

The Rider moved back over to the cowering couple and bent down, resting his elbows on his knees, squatting so that he was just a head above the two, as if he were watching over them in protection. He lifted his hat from where it rested on the floor and placed it on his head. His eyes were thrown even more into shadow now, the white shimmering hesitantly under its covering.

"I keep that balance of life and death," he said. "Revenge is a wasteful process. Has been since the beginning. That ain't why I'm here. I am not my brother's keeper. The Lord says that vengeance is his. I only act upon his messages. For the God of vengeance and of spite is still in possession of our souls, still reignin."

The man tried to stand but he fell down with each attempt. His wife sat still, letting the tears pool on the floor below her. Her hands twitched violently, as if she were trying to grab hold of something that flew too quickly between her fingers. She looked over to her husband and then up to The Rider. A sob broke from her throat and she looked back to her husband; in his eyes she could see a strange peace or acceptance, and this comforted her somehow. Though she did not know why. And she breathed deep and stretched her arm out so that her hand laid gently on her husband's.

The Rider drew his long coat aside and brought out his long knife from its sheath. He watched as the reflection of the spreading fire behind him glistened off the blade. His eyes moved to the silent strangers in front of him. He breathed in deeply, smelling the dark aroma of the world around him. It was in moments such as these, when he held the killing instrument tightly in his hand, that he knew he was destined and cursed to walk the world, a zealot in his own mind, like some recipient of salvation given to him by a faceless preacher in a revival inhabited only by grotesques and degenerates. He was exiled to a wandering life of indentured servitude. He knew this. And so it was.

Josiah had just finished balancing the doe's body on the saddle on top of the horse. The head of the lifeless animal was thrown back, its eyes lolled white and its tongue stuck out from the corner of its mouth. Its soft brown hide was stained red on its neck from where the bullet had entered and, passing through, exited on the other side. The blood had dried and was now only a crusted reminder of the life that had escaped. The boy walked to the front of the horse and stroked the soft bristled hair between the animal's eyes and then he grabbed the leathered reins and slowly led the horse toward home.

Even though the sun had sunk over the ridged skyline hours before, Josiah could still hear the constant buzzing of flies and mosquitoes trying to suckle from the raw and bloodied body of the doe. The path stretched on for miles as the two—boy and horse—walked silently: neither led, neither followed. The boy allowed his mind to meander about as the wind rushed unsettlingly through the woods. His eyes were fixed on the dark road ahead, watching the shadowed figures of the trees scattered before him, lurking above in silent revelry. And he below them, leading the horse over stream and under star.

After they had walked for an hour or so, Josiah heard in the near distance the neighing call of a horse and the plodding muffle of the animal's feet clambering over the ground. The boy and his horse stopped moving and he listened in the still air, searching for sign of the animal. He held his breath and after a while his chest began to hurt. Then he saw it: through the trees and cresting over the hill before him some two hundred yards away, a horse ran. It was black, he could tell. The horse was graceful and moved at a fast pace in his direction. Josiah followed its movements, watching it approach. The dark horse rode past the two silent figures, coming within a few yards from them, and in the starlight Josiah could see that, like the horse, its rider was cloaked in black. The boy studied The Rider as he passed, believing that he looked to be Death himself. And then, as quickly and peaceably as the horse was heard and The Rider seen, they both disappeared and the horizon was quiet and all was as it once was.

Josiah started walking forward again. He tugged at the reins of the horse, stirring it from its short respite. They moved in steady order, these two creatures, their eyes shifting up to the sky and back to the ground, each feeling subtly misplaced, as if something were changed, something different this night from before, something new or, worse yet, something lost. Gone. They moved forward, and their searching eyes gave them the illusion of pacifist pilgrims journeying to some savage and treacherous place, a place once recognizable but now eradicated of all familiarity and comfort. He looked behind him every so often, but would always return his gaze forward as he soldiered forward into that new and unholy land.

William Corvin awoke in the middle of the night. He looked over and saw Maria lying naked on the bed beside him. Beautiful, innocent, vulnerable. Her black hair was swirled in a mass, surrounding and entrapping her face. Her skin was a deep brown in the flickering candlelight, her breasts rising and falling gently with each breath, lips twitching with each dream.

He reached his hand across to her and stroked the back of his hand down her cheek, feeling the warmth and softness of her skin in the cooling night. He smiled and then slowly, making sure not to wake her, stood and walked out of the room and down the hall of the large house, gazing briefly up at the painted portraits of his family line hanging upon the walls—guardians of past times—and he turned from their eyes as he walked, feeling as if they continued to watch him, judging him even still.

Corvin walked through the dining room, its table and chairs gleaming in the darkness, the room illuminated only by the glow of candlelight in the far-off corner of the house—a section reserved for the maids and cooks and workers from his father's time and before. But now there was no one save himself and Maria. Jefferson still spent his nights in the barn. Corvin had asked Jefferson to sleep in the house when they returned home, but the old black man had refused every time he was asked and Corvin had since given up asking.

From the dining room, he walked to the old servants' rooms in the rear of the house, where the candles burned low, and he made his way slowly down the six steps that separated these rooms from the entry level of the house. He paused briefly on these steps and listened. The depths of the house still seemed alive to him with years of memories and the burdened footsteps of countless people—children, parents, servants—long dead now. He continued down the steps. Before him were four small rooms, each no larger than the next, each able to hold three sleeping men or women. He walked past these rooms; in one of them he heard the slow measuring canter of a clock slowly ticking away the time: the present was becoming the past, the future the present, and the past a forgotten thing altogether.

Just beyond these small rooms, Corvin opened a door that led out into the rear yard of the house and he walked out, closing the door gently. The yard lay before him, a dark sea in the night air. He imagined if he looked close enough he might see the ships of some foreign explorer, the kinds he had read about as a child. But he did not look and the sea remained calm.

He looked above him, measuring himself to the stars, placing himself against them. The air surrounding him felt cool against his bare chest, a thin layer of sweat the only thing covering his skin. He stood on a large wooden porch that stretched several feet out beyond the roof and surrounded the house in its entirety like a moat begging to be crossed by some stranger of the distant past that had all but been dismissed from recollection. A wood railing ran along the end of the porch and he walked the perimeter of the house, letting his hand glide along this wood rail.

He made his way to the front of the house and walked down the set of wooden steps that connected the heavy front door to the yard. Out to his right, wading in the dark sea, was the barn and just beyond and to the right of this was the stable where four horses were kept.

Corvin slowly descended the three steps and stood now on the kindled shavings and clipped wood of trees and stones scattered now, leaves and grass forever resigned to stay etched in a pathway, immovable and worn by years past. Beyond the yard stretched the secreted alcoves and hidden meadows of the woods and he searched the darkness for signs of life but found none that he could see. But life did exist out there in the night. He could hear it—the constant screeching of cicadas and palmetto bugs, their bodies blacker still against the black trees. These insects' sounds had always been a comfort to him, a way to keep from complete isolation. Corvin closed his eyes and listened to their voices, hundreds combining and overlapping each other, all of them creating a strange harmony, calling out in warning of some storm that had not come yet, or possibly it had and they were only lamenting for what they had already lost.

Corvin opened his eyes and turned to the house and looked upon the figure of stone and wood, the shaded windows. He could smell the saccharine scent of her sweat on his skin. He knelt to the ground, letting his knees become dampened and cold on the earth. He took a deep breath and let it out slowly. He no longer feared the coming days. He had not yet become accustomed to it, even after being home with her for two years. He closed his eyes and let his mind drift back to when he first saw her in that room, the cold steel against his skin and her face dancing before him like a mirage.

He had found something within her that he could not understand or explain. He had laid down the binding restraints of anger and fear that he had felt of this place. It had, all at once, become something new again. He found hope, he thought, and, in it, he found absolution. He opened his eyes and stood. From his back pocket he pulled forth a bent and flimsy tintype photograph and he studied it. He knew the image by memory, but he looked at it as if it were the first time he had seen it. He held the thing tightly in his hand, the fingers of his other hand gently caressed the face of the woman it showed. He took a deep breath and then exhaled slowly and replaced the tintype in his back pocket, back to where he carried it with him always.

He turned from the silhouette of the house and looked off to the east. Even from the miles of separation, he could smell the acrid and raw stench of the mine shafts. He could see the dust clouds and the blackened ground, the shards and pieces of coal and mica that the mines spewed, all fluttering wildly in the breeze.

He could hear the horses being lashed together and the whipping that drew them in the march forward, the sound of the wheels on the steel rails as the carts were brought up with their nightblack cargo. The steady sound of metal against rock coming from the holes that stretched into and under the hills and mountains.

On the dark horizon he could feel the heat of the locomotive engine, its grinding gears. He could see the machine leaving from the small station in Eliott, the black earth being carried north to be delivered to the factories and distributors who would transfer the allotted amount into the bank account his grandfather had established years before. And so the cycle would continue just as it had for his father and his father's father before him.

Corvin stopped and looked out toward and past the shadowed mass of trees. The valley stretched about in all directions as far as he could see. In the valley floor, cleared of trees and life, he thought he could make out the barely perceptible amber glow of flamed light coming from the minecamp.

Corvin imagined the workers huddled within their shacked lodges, trying in some unabled way to dream relief from the rigors of the day before the tomorrow began and that routined life of theirs started again. Their stinging and drowsy eyes still not used to the freshness of the air, hurting them as they shut the lids of their eyes tightly, their hands black and raw and calloused from the picks and hammers that they held all day—their fingers would be cupped and remain so, holding the phantom tool. In their sleep they might even continue working, their hands moving forward, knocking personal belongings from their bedside tables, pictures and letters. They would sleep and dream of ghosts walking the woodlands that surrounded them, these phantoms calling out for lost loves dead and gone centuries ago.

Corvin had heard the talks of strike in Pennsylvania and other parts of the country, but he did not worry himself with these rumors.

He breathed out again, this time noticing the faint fog that came from his breath, and he turned back to the house. Inside, everything was calm and quiet. Peaceful in the dark night.

Like some pagan exiting from a land wholly removed from existence, Josiah made his way to the outskirts of the woods toward the clearing. He was still leading the horse on foot, still balancing the doe on the horse's back. The small cabinhouse was resting in the keep of this clearing, sitting just beyond the small hill before him past and through these trees. Behind him, the steady and manacled sound of slow dripping liquid falling on the earth's floor seemed to resonate all about him, echoing off the trees above him and over the assortment of dead and dying leaves and spent kindling below his feet. The blood trail followed behind them from the creek. The doe's head was still slung back in its dead call.

As they walked to the bottom of the hill, the perfumed intoxicant of smoke filled the boy's nostrils and stung his lungs before he could see the carnage. He slowly led the horse up the hill, his breathing becoming short. The animal nervously twitched and pulled back towards the comfort of the woods. The reins burned the boy's hands as the animal jerked its head this way and that, lifting up on its two hind legs and then bringing his front ones back down in a crash of overpowering angst, trying in a misled belief that it could break free from what they soon would behold. The doe slid from the horse's back and dropped heavily on the earth. Josiah didn't look back at the carcass; he kept moving up the hill toward whatever awaited him.

His footsteps became slow and chopped, his head down, studying the way his booted feet landed on the rocky ground. He noticed the melancholy sound of the loose rocks colliding with one another; they sounded as if they were talking to themselves in a speech that really talked to no one at all. He looked up to the ridge of the hill above him and saw the faint glow. Light in a dark world, entangling and mesmerizing an onlooker in the innocence and splendor of its color.

When he reached the top of the hill he beheld what he knew all along he would find: the sight surreal even to his expecting eyes. Before him stood the back of the cabinhouse, normally a silhouette in the dark but now a dancing and blazing composition left to smolder out in a time all its own. The incandescence flooding itself from off the dirt ground now reddened and blackened from the smoke and flame. The tongued licks of orange and yellow and red stretched upward and disappeared in the cooling night air. A blue arabesque haze seemed to encircle the burning wood of the house that was dilapidating in itself and falling down in one compost heap, sobered now from the night and its dealings. It was as if the fire was consuming itself in its own calm rapture. Forgotten now were the events that played themselves out before the flames took their hold. The only thing left to remember was the destruction.

The boy slowly led the horse, now calmed from its nervous confusion, around the side of the flaming house. He noted where his small room once was and he watched the planks of wood that were now being consumed in the devastation of the hellish fire.

He stopped and looked upon the house from the clearing in front of the smoldering structure. The steps of the house had all but been incinerated, fallen down now in black remains to become part of the earth once more. The front door had fallen from where it stood and was still flaming.

Josiah turned to the wooded grove behind him. It was calm and quiet. He began to walk toward it, noticing a swaying movement in the trees encompassing the place. Safety and comfort no more. He hid the sight of the desolation behind him by keeping his gaze on the dark trees. He let the reins fall slowly from his cut and bruised hands leaking blood from torn skin, his hands still clamped and cramped shut from his grip on the leather. The horse ran in the direction they had come, around the side of the house and down the hill.

He took a few steps, his eyes fixed upward to the abysmal keep of the stars through the shade of the branches. He stumbled over the heavy weight of something lying in the dirty ground at his feet. His body tensed and a cold chill streaked itself throughout his spine and fingertips as he looked at his feet and what he had kicked. The dark body of the dog, sloughed and lifeless in the night, lay. Blood was dried about its neck and around its head on the dirt ground. Worms and flies were already searching the body. He bent and touched the fur of the animal, now cold and coarse, and stood and continued to the trees. The trees seemed to flutter back and forth as if whispering some hidden secret to each other, diabolical and gentle all at once.

As he advanced, he could see a set of dark shadows, a serene malediction in the dignified and gnarled arms and fingers of the trees. He slowed his walk, a pit beginning to rise in his stomach, sweat beading and bursting forth from his skin; cold in the black air. He stopped several yards from the woods, the trees stretching endlessly before him, circling around behind him, creeping ever-so-gently upon him in a comforting cataclysm. He looked up to the shadows on the treeline, watching the two figures gently swirl in the breeze, the rope creaking noisily as the bodies swayed left, then right, then left again. The eidetic scene was thrown into a dreamlike miasma by the quick glow from the fire behind, harshly showering the landscape in a reality of light, then throwing the panorama back into a darkness before letting the light come again, an ember in the vast centrifuges of the world.

The wilted bodies of his mother and father hanged from the trees, their feet suspended in space and time by the rope. Twisting gently and methodically above him.

Josiah dropped his sight to the ground and saw the two puddles of dark blood pooling and mixing with each other on the ground below. In the flickering light he could see the skin melted and hanging down off the bones of the faces. His father's arms and his mother's legs had lost all the skin and now only showed of blackened bone and muscle, a ghastly hint of tarred skin frayed and formless. His father's chest held an aureate glow that washed itself in the night. On each of their faces, he could see the trail of slashes circling around the eye-sockets containing no eyes; they had been removed, an infectious disease wishing itself to be abolished, its antibody found, yet its symptoms remained untreated. The deep gaping cavities of the eye-sockets looked out upon a destruction hidden away in some prescriptive darkness; they stared in awed bewilderment at the ominous display before them, the flames twisting and twirling, running about the scene in a forayed commotion like soldiers or children, or both.

He turned and sat on the ground and watched the devastation of the house. The gentle creak of the ropes on the limbs of the trees above him and the steady crackling of the wood within the fire played together in a melody of death and annihilation, a symphony of pain and remorse orchestrated in the fiery bowels of the earth.

He brought his legs up close under him and cried. Through his tears, he looked at the woods around him, feeling their tender breath on his nape. The trees loomed in the tranquility of the night air, an amalgamation of the past and present gently swaying in unison within the evening's cool breeze, summoning within its deep recesses the dawn of the future and the events that were foreshadowed since the beginning of time.

The Rider

What is life but a series of meetins and greetins and farewells and goodbyes strung together by some higher callin unknown from ourselves? It all leads us to some eventual knowin of one another, I imagine. And only then can we really hope to understand ourselves. That's what I think, at least. I've come to see that life is truly one choice after the other. And still I have been appointed the job of decidin what choices are right. It was what I was told along the shore of the lake that day. Years ago. What she told me. There's better ways of handlin a horse thief, I find. But they made their choice. And they paid for it in the only currency that means anythin in life. In blood. It's all we truly got . . . I'm an orphan. By choice, mind you. That's how it was in the beginnin too. Just me. Alone. In the dark of nothin. Without knowin it, I returned my present bein to that state. My actions, my choices, my will . . . To start would be to tell of my parents. They were both drunk more than they were sober. Always saturated with the poison, seepin it like a venom through their skin, their pores leakin it so that their stench was a combination: a sweetness and a bitter sour. You could smell it. They were the dirty filth of the this world. The kind I was appointed to destroy. The kind I would vow to rid, to exterminate and cleanse this world . . . Lots of them puppets out there, just like my parents. They'd come home each night with moonshine and whiskey, rotgut in them and start slappin at each other. When they got tired of that they'd wake me and start in on me. Always somethin. Every night, never failin. Every mornin I'd wake and wash the blood off my skin from the night prior, lick my wounds like a dog. Sometimes I'd cry, but then I'd brace myself for the next night, and the next, and the next. Life. I lived in the shadow of a fear I never understood . . . My father was a ranch hand over near Clarksview. He wasn't around much for lots of the year. Probably was best he wasn't. My mother did what she did, I guess. Never knew much about her. Never wanted to. She'd sleep til twelve noon some days, most days, snorin and congestin the air with her polluted breath and stale skin odor. On most nights when he was away she'd bring them by. And I'd watch through the slats in the walls and see them all cut up into sections. Light then dark then light then dark. She would lie still all the while and they would leave the money on the table when they left . . . I would always make my way down to the river's edge, right there where the willow trees hang over the water, and I'd sit and think about life—read my Bible mostly. The preacher gave it to me one Sunday after the service. He smiled, and it was the last true smile I can remember. The trees and the wind, the animals—deer and rabbits mostly, birds some of the time—they would keep me company. Never trusted no man or woman in those early days. Still don't. I'd breathe in the air, never smell of alcohol. It was free. Alive and pure. So pure. I longed for that purity. And in that heaven of mine, secluded from time and place of the world and its evils, I'd read from that holy book. Believed myself to be born there. Never understood the words in the book much when I was young, but then again I never understood life and the cruelty of people. Their foulness and filth. They disgusted me. And I'd sit there and feel better when I saw the words. I'd think a lot about my place and my situation, my life. Never could understand how I could hate so much the people who birthed me into this world. I never saw me as one of them, I reckon. I wasn't part of them, as I was told children were of their parents. I was somethin else . . . Many of those days I'd wonder about God. And, on those days down there, after all that thinkin I'd usually fall asleep next to the water's edge. And I would dream.

2

The world seems void of color now. It sits still, awaiting some master-creator's colored brush strokes. The shadows lay dormant and the silhouettes of trees and animals can be seen against the backdrop of the night. And then slowly, in some unknown progression that we may never understand, the morning light casts off the darkness and vanishes those incubi and succubi of the night.

This is a warmer morning than has been for some time, at least since the season began its change. Many of the people say quietly that it will snow soon, but first the rains must come. They must come and slowly usher in the snows like a nurse or doctor would an infirmed patient, and then there will be snow and cold and death.

Stretching to the ends of this earth are the lines and rows and clusters of trees—maple and oak and cedar and others—that seem to stretch their twisted bodies upward. The tips of these beings still hold some color, and this color of orange and red and yellow and still some green shines in the morning light and seems to direct this light through their prism and cast it about the ground in a translucence. To look over these treetops from above is to witness a phoenix of color arising from some long deceased flame where ashes have gone cold and flaked. And these leaves, which cling to the tops of these trees, seem to do so as if they are holding on to some dying wish of life and existence that soon will be relinquished with their eventual and steady fall to the earth and their unheralded burial within the dirt.

And a cool breeze begins now, and in its revival of the leaves, those fallen and those still attached at their stems, you can just begin to make out the deep soliloquies of the past—Listen! They are calling out, telling us what they have seen and what they wish never to see again.

They all sat still, hushed in a reverence that seemed to echo about and consume the small and dusty chapel. The splintering floorboards remained quiet. A whispered semblance of grief seemed to hang about the wooden room, encircling each member, confining each. From afar they would have looked like iron clad idols formed by some immaculate creator and arranged just so. And they all sat unmoving, unaware of their purpose. Their heads were bowed and eyes closed in quiet reflection of the day's trials, of life's passings; the steady dinned tick of life and death tolled away around each man or woman, allowing the days to slip from night to morning, then to dusk, before the ancient cycle repeated itself. And then, as suddenly as a bird's call in a white winter, the minister began.

"Death is our only escape from life. It is God's way of offering hope within a land made hopeless by the sins and transgressions and wickedness of the evil and the depraved. The search for reason in death drives us all forward through our days here, in life." He paused and looked around the room, to the congregants before him. The sounds from outside played through the open door in the back of the room and surrounded them all in the small place. He closed his eyes and continued: "What is this world but a mere stop on the way to our true lives? We inhabit this body of ours in order to merely test ourselves and each other. It is God's judgment that will reign supreme as he observes us every day from our birth into this world to the day of our birth into the next. Today, we simple people gather together to witness and to celebrate a birth into immortality and paradise."

The minister opened his eyes slowly and cautiously, quietly, as if some imposing corporeal being stood before him, waiting to strike him down. He glanced upon the faces before him. The heads of the men were all removed of hats, hair slicked back and shining in the candlelight surrounding them.

Meandering rays of sunlight penetrated the loose slits and cracks of wood from the ceiling and the walls, giving an ethereal ambiance to the place. The napes of the men were scarlet, the faces white from hiding from the sun all day under wide brims; grime and oil grease and the blackness of earth still resided on their cracking skin; their fingers were swollen and jagged and calloused, fingernails broken and black. The women all sat in their simple white and black or all black dresses, some fanning their pasty white skin, others sitting peaceably, hands folded and set in the lap.

The pews were lined in rows. They were made of a worn wood that looked rotted and broken down, and as each person shifted his or her weight the wood would let out loud groans and other sounds of wear. The body was segregated: men to the left side, women to the right. Each congregant's body was placed in succession to the one before it, each lolled head arranged in some meaningless pattern, all ordered except for the man standing at the pulpit, stationed before the small congregation.

Corvin opened his eyes and focused his attention on the minister, who stood clad in a black vestment that stretched down from his neck to his feet, the fabric beginning to corrugate itself around this man's upraised arms. Sweat was forming under the dark fabric of the chest and sleeves. The minister's eyes were now closed again, his head not bowed as the others but was raised up, searching beyond the closed lids, through the dark, mildewed wooden ceiling above, into the firmament of oblivion for some existential answer. This man, this minister of God. His dark hair now matted on his pale scalp. His arms shook gently under the strain of their uplifted pose, a nervous twitch rushing through his body, coursing through his hands and outstretched fingers.

Next to the podium where the minister stood was a wooden box of some six feet in length. A small collection of flowers were grouped together and placed on the box's lid. Corvin looked about the room and again closed his eyes, losing himself once more in the starry darkness of his mind's perception. The minister lowered his arms and opened his eyes and spoke again.

"Times of loss require us all to question ourselves, ask ourselves what it is we live for. Why we breathe? What is it that makes us awaken each morning and venture into a world of sin? Along with the questions we should remind ourselves of the answer. It's a simple answer—it is the knowledge of a guiding light. One that shows us through the inescapable darkness of sin and hate. This knowledge and our acceptance of this knowledge begins the road to salvation for each of us; it allows us to navigate this world, our eyes steady on the one that awaits.

"Although Samantha MacAdams was only in this world for six brief years, it was evident that she held that knowledge. God's light shined brightly on her. Anyone could see it. Jesus tells us that the pure of heart see God and are with him for eternity. Now she sits before him. Among him." He looked about the room quickly and then continued. "God tells those who mourn that they will be comforted. And we are here today mourning her so that we will be comforted. It is only together and with God alone that we shall comfort ourselves in the hope of salvation."

The minister's voice continued on in the musty room, but Corvin didn't listen; he couldn't hear the minister anymore. Instead, he allowed his mind to wander to the woman seated across the room from where he sat. Maria's dark hand nestled within his keep, protecting it, comforting him in the darkness of the world. The gentle touch. Light of possibility; blinding rays of redemption. And he smiled.

The ground was hard and smelled of sulfur. Josiah lay on his back, his head cradled against the saddle, and counted the stars until he allowed is eyes to close and let sleep overtake him.

In his dreams he could hear his mother. The reckless scraping sound of a spoon on a greased pan echoed about in a soothing evanescence within the enclosure of the house, keeping a metronomed beat with the susurrations of the wind outside. He could see his father, slowly rocking in his chair, the creak of the wood sounding him in the dim room. The old man's eyes were closed. And then all was silent.

In his dream, the boy stood rigid. Unmoving. Rebelling against the natural laws of both reality and the mind. Time itself was suspended, the birds lost in the shuffled stillness of the world outside. Silent. Silent. He watched with a drowsy intensity as his mother dropped the pan and spoon, both rattling on the floor without sound. Silent still. Still. She turned to face him, her eyes closed also. She seemed to be staring at him without sight. He felt his body become weightless, his mind free of expectation. He was without conviction in the convicting realm of truth. His feet lifted off the ground, his eyes raised upward. His arms stretched out in equal height and direction—outward; level. His shadow bled itself onto the ground below him. A cross maybe; he couldn't tell. The dream played on. Silent still all about him.

Then, like an erumpent force breaking the crystalline clarity of the silence, he could hear the staggered screams of the multitudes outside. They called his name in their muted and hushed tones, their voices blending within one another until they became one voice, beckoning him onward, offering a stalwart supplication from him, seeking salvation and alleviation from their pains—their copious desire of life. Their hope in the uncertain. The boy's eyes dropped back down to his parents—their lids were still closed, hiding from the world the buried secrets beneath. His heart throbbed painfully in his chest. His feet still hovered above the ground. He reached to his chest, scratching, tearing at the flesh. The roar of the crowds outside the door grew louder and louder: more pleading now, more forceful now, calling him, imploring his grace of salvation until he closed his own eyes. Then all was quiet again.

When Josiah opened his eyes he found the familiar patterns of the stars welcoming him back. In the distance he heard the scattered shuffle of a raccoon rustling through the low hanging branches and over dried and dead leaves fallen from the oncoming winter. The sounds of the insects seemed to consume the night sky and surround him. The hazy glow from the embers of the fire next to him had all but disappeared. He wasn't cold but he shivered. He stood uneasily and began to search the ground, squinting in the dark light of the stars for kindling and wood. He walked to where his horse stood and stroked his hand gently down the side of the animal, patting it softly, speaking to it in cooing hushes. He drew the blanket higher on the horse and then continued on, bending every once and again to pick up a stick or log, each time wincing in stiffness from the riding of the past few days. He had become tired from wandering aimlessly about in the vastness of the world that was his own. And he had no direction, no path of which to follow.

Although he was far removed from his house and the swinging bodies of his parents he could still smell smoke in the air, a reminder of the past, a lingering taste of it on his tongue. Trees danced in the faint glow of what was left of the fire behind him, their shadows moving and talking to each other in communion with the rest of nature, seemingly discussing the existence of the boy and his place amongst them. They were scattered unevenly, here and there, closing in on the boy, surrounding him. Either protecting or threatening, neither the boy nor the trees seemed to know which.

His hands were full when he started to make his way back to his camp, navigating the bases of the trees like people in a crowd. In the distance, not far from where the fire was dying down in the night, he saw the slow bob of an ethereal light, nodding and winking, dipping up and then down, swinging left to right in the darkness. Hovering in the night. He set the wood pieces down and ran quietly and rigidly to where his horse stood, its head bowed down as if praying to a god in the shadows, one hidden in the bowels of the night. As the boy approached, the horse drew its head up brusquely and began to flail it about impatiently. The boy hushed the horse and reached to the ground where he had been sleeping, feeling the dirt with his fingertips, his eyes still on the moving light beyond the clearing, kept within the trees, winking every once and again as it moved behind something, disappearing momentarily and then reappearing as if it had never gone away. His fingers brushed against the long metallic frame and he picked up the rifle and scampered forward. Toward the light, to the intruders of the dark.

As the shaft of light came closer, Josiah slowed to a trot. Then a walk. His breath was heavy, escaping itself in rough bursts, lingering for only the briefest of time in the cold of the night and then dissipating into the essence of what it had ultimately been born from. His nose was dripping and he tried to wipe away the liquid mucus from his upper lip but it only returned as soon as his hand left his face. He hid behind a tree, the wood now gnarled from its years of existence. Josiah peeked his head slightly around the limbs, watching the light. He held his breath and listened. Silence in his mind. A steady pain rose within the boy's chest, beating his ribs, straining his inner body. He let his breath out slowly once more, trying not to awaken the demons or angels of the night.

He leveled the barrel toward the glowing phantom and inched closer, his feet clumsily snapping brush and crackling kindled wood. His breath was even now, quiet. He moved farther into the enclosure of the trees' surrounds and positioned himself in front of the oncoming ghost, kneeling behind a log. Thorns and thistles and needles and brambles and briars all fallen from the tree tops dug themselves into his leg. The rocky ground bruised his knee as he knelt, but still he waited. The light seemed to dance alone, not moving forward but rather steadying itself in a slow march in place. A faceless luminary of the night. Without feeling. Without identity. Without fear.

He waited in the stillness of his own mind. Time seemed to creep past without acknowledgment, slowly moving at its own pace. It allowed those consumed by it to choose: follow or be passed by. A reflected face in glass. He set the gun on the ground and rubbed his hands together, blowing periodically into them, clenching and releasing his fists, then taking the gun up once more. After a while he sat, his back pushed against the wood of the log. A breeze wailed gently through the night. A shewolf's call, summoning the forces of existence and creating some preordained counterpoint to his feeling of abandoned grief and loss. His eyes closed and in the darkness he could remember the dream. He could hear the chanting from without his house, the slow drone of voices converging into one. A cacophony of muted sound merging with grace and steadiness in the depths of dusk. "Save us. Save us," they had called to him. Over and over, repeated, humming with the sound of the wind. Their voices were intertwined and held immobile within their own impassioned call. He pulled his coat tighter to his body. It smelled of his father.

Sound ruptured through the covering of the trees and the boy opened his eyes and listened. A crackle. Wood snapping under foot. Silence and then a rustle before silence once more. Josiah heard a man's deep voice hushing in the night. "Shhh." The voice spoke nothing else. He could hear the padded footsteps without prints treading in the darkness of life. Blind. Alone. Silent. He picked up the rifle and held it tight, the cold steel brushing against his face, the barrel upright, aiming at the darkened sky above. His head emerged from behind the log stump that was his protection. He leveled the barrel once more at the light, his finger already pressing in upon the trigger. His eyes twitched and he blinked quickly to calm them.

The light was not distanced from him by more than several steps, and Josiah watched as the flamed torch slowly passed by where he was. He then saw the spirits that followed the light's directed lead. In the flicker of the flame he could make out the silhouetted outline of a negro man, clothes ragged and ripped, his body caked in dirt and other foulness. This man carried the flame high, a truncheon against the maladies of the world; the light a single redeemer. Prometheus's gift and his own curse. The man's face was hard and set and dark, seeping and mixing with the night's painted strokes, becoming, all at once, the same and separate from the masquerade that was the life that embodied and surrounded him.

Josiah could see the man stop and turn, then turn back to where he walked. He continued on. Behind the man was a woman, her body nonexistent save for the white sheets wrapped around her head and the swashes of white cotton on her clothing. Behind her were three young children; in the darkness their bodies were mere specters rather than ones created of flesh. These people were ghosts in the devil's own land, unaware of what lay ahead. They continued on slowly in some wanderlust to which the boy remained outside and set apart.

The boy let the gun slowly slide from his grip and he set it once more on the ground. He followed the light until it was consumed in the woods ahead, watching these people pass in their furtive quietness. Simply existing as such.

And deep in the faint solitude of the woods, an owl called.

That same night, far removed from the boy and the place where he lay, a bonfire raged in the deep wilderness where the arms of trees and plants and rocky cliffs loomed and seemed to invade the peaceful recesses of the land. A throng of men and women, their bodies naked and covered only in strips of animal flesh, danced around the caldera that lit this small portion of the earth.

They danced and sang out into the dark ether of the night. A pagan revival comprised of grotesques and degenerates and ghouls in full human war paint, their shadows reflecting over the dark land and stretching past the rock-strewn distance like rubber stretched too taut and thin, almost breaking under the strain. On their faces were streaks of blood and dirt, their skin was turned a gruesome black in the night so that only their eyes and their teeth could be seen. In the bedlam of the scene, a man's voice rang high above the others and called out, and this voice carried over the land only to disappear somewhere entirely removed from where he now stood. Soon the entire congregation was silent and all eyes were fixed on this one man whose arms were raised to the sky like a supplicant to the universe. After some time, he stopped his cries and reached to the earth and picked up a knife carved from stone and wood and slowly drew the blade across his palm and then squeezed his fist tightly. The others merely watched, a quiet tenseness settling about them all. The man walked to the flames and clenched his grip tighter and let the thin stream of blood fall into the fire to be swallowed by the flames.

From afar, two thieving men watched this ceremony. Neither talked. They each lay on their stomachs and looked on at the scene before them, and after some unknown time of quiet the men heard the cries of joy or pain—they could not decipher which—from the crowd, and then they looked at each other and crept off, leaving the horde to itself, and they disappeared into the dark.

The sun arose brightly in the clear morning, pushing away the ghosts and dreams and memories from the night before. The Rider swung down from the horse and tied the animal to the post and walked into the small saloon and took a seat at the bar. He scratched at the stubble on his cheek and looked down at the dried blood on his pant leg. The man behind the counter set out a glass on the wood between the two and asked the man what he'd drink.

"Water, please. Cold water."

The man behind the counter turned and filled the glass while The Rider took off his long black coat, dusty and smelling of soot and flame, and set it on the chair next to him. He took off his hat and set it on top of the bundled coat. "Quiet in here," The Rider said, looking about the room. The counter at which he sat was raised above the floor of the main room by two steps. From here, the barkeep could survey the whole of the room—the commotions and card games, arguments and handshakes, smiles and drunken staggering of men wasting away their lives in pursuit of some elusive hand dealt by chance or fortune or luck or God, each shunning their very existence in the darkness of the shadows of the room.

On the floor were several tables with empty seats; burn marks from cigarettes and cigars and yellowing mold from spilled alcohol ornamented the floor beneath the wooden chairs. In the corner was a decaying woodbox piano, become derelict from years of melodies and ages of harmonies. It was silent now. The candlelight leaking from lanterns hung randomly from the high ceiling above flickered in and out in the stale air, and the sunlight flooded inside the room in slow swallowed gasps through the naked glass windows that looked out at a tranquil street of a quiet and lived in town. It was a place too old for the advent of electricity, a town still rooted firmly in the ways of what once was, as if it were shunning modernity in some fear of inescapable novelty. The piano's shadow spilled over the ground, the deep darkness reaching like fingers inward towards the two men at the bar, the shadow retreating from the hazed light as if the illumination carried with it a death plague unknown to humans.

The instrument seemed to blend into the wood sidings of the room. Above, hanging from a balcony that stretched the length and perimeter of the room, were red fabric sheets ruffled and stretched and turned a dusty burgundy from smoke and time. They had been put there to give some romantic charm to the place, as if the walls that they covered were to be ignored, or rather yet hidden from the world in disappointment. The Rider looked to the balcony, noticing the dented and rotting wood of the handrails. On the balcony he could see doors shut to the outside, concealing some mischievous exercise within, some exclusive séance that the closed wood held secret.

"You got many girls here?" The Rider asked, turning back to the barman.

"Some. Got eight in all," the barman said, turning with a glass full of water. His eyes squinted and hid themselves behind a pair of small glasses. His hair was greased back, parted slightly in the middle and curling up unevenly at the sides. He tried not to look at the seated man's left eye, the long scar circling and stretching the length of the man's face. He looked away. "Most of them're out or sleepin now. We maybe got one or two up now and ready yet. Though the night's popular with them. You could come back then, or I reckon I can go get one up for you?" The barman looked up at The Rider. "You want me to?" he asked, wiping his hands on the front of his shirt. The barman smiled.

The Rider raised the glass and drank from it and then set it back down on the counter. He tried to fit the edges of the glass within the ring of watered residue from its earlier position. "No need. If it's meant to be, she'll come, I suppose. I'll see later."

"You from round here?" The barman brought his hand up and smoothed the black hair above his lip, a thick, dark line of a moustache.

"No." Another sip from the glass. Another tick of it set against the wood.

"Where you from?"

"Nowhere."

"Drifter?" The man wiped his hands on his shirt again and then busied himself with a rag on the wood counter. "Not that it makes no difference to me."

"No. I know where I'm headed. I know where I come from too. If you know that then I suppose you ain't much of a drifter. You think?"

"Can't say really." He looked up at the man across from him. "Where you headed then?"

"All the same. You're born, then you die. Raised from ash, sent back into ash. Faithful and unfaithful alike. We're all of the earth; all except when we're on it."

"You a preacher?"

"No sir." The Rider wiped his hands on his pants, the palm grazing the knife and pistols set on his belt. "No sir. I am what is preached."

"That so?"

"It is so." He took another drink. He smiled.

The barman wiped his mouth and then turned to face the collection of bottles, some with labels on the glass, some of the stickers falling and peeling, other bottles simply a milky clear or brown glass. He set the rag down and wiped his face, the sweat beaded on his skin now gone; he wiped his hand on his shirt. He turned and looked at the man seated—his eyes lost in the reddened scar and bristled hair below it.

"I ain't some crazed fool. I know that look," The Rider said. "I'm sane." He drank. "You lookin at this here," he traced the line of the mark with his blackened and dusty finger, the chipped and earthen nails dark against his skin before blending in and becoming lost in the stubble of a beard.

"No, sir. I ain't."

"Maybe you weren't, but now you are. Right?" The Rider smiled.

"Maybe. I suppose now. Don't mean nothing by it, though. Sorry to offend you."

"It's all right. Got it a long time ago. Didn't feel a thing when it happened. Just the blood runnin down. It was a sign to me then. Still is."

"How'd it happen?"

"A thing of the past. Can't remember much of it now."

The barman slowly dropped his head and studied the spots and smudges on the wood, the dark marks on it blending to one.

"You read the Bible?" The Rider let his fingers gently play with the butt of the knife at his side.

"No. Not much, I guess. You sure you ain't no preacher, huh?"

"Not by trade. By default, I guess you could say. Defendin the Word is all. My purpose. I found that when I got this here cut. It's important—maybe the most important thing: to find your purpose. If you're lost to yourself, then you're lost to all mankind. You find your direction, though, then you can be somethin. Somethin true and right. You can perform the miracles of this world without even knowin it. You find your purpose yet?"

The barman smiled and looked up at the man across from him. "Can't say I have yet."

"That's a shame. Time runs short for you. Before you know it you'll be facin your judgment."

"I guess."

"You guess." The Rider leaned back on his stool. He smiled and stood and walked along the bar, running his hand on the smooth wood, noting the cool luster of it. The obscured glow from the outside light through the window cast a nebulous indistinction on the patterns and mazes of the wood. "You own this place?"

"In a way. Owner up and run off a while back. Some men out to get him. Just kinda fell down to me."

"You still showin the girls regular?"

"Ain't nothin changed when he left. They're still here. I'm still here."

"I forgot. How many you say you got in the house right now?"

"Eight right now. Got a couple really good ones, too. One especially. Nice piece, that one."

"You get good money from them all?"

"Ain't much polite in sayin it, but yeah. There's plenty in it."

"Don't feel bad doin it? Holdin them here? Makin profit opposin God's word?"

"Ain't *that* much profit in it. I guess I haven't really considered it none. I keep them girls good though; they ain't mistreated." He took his small glasses from off their narrow perch and wiped them on his shirtfront. "But then again, they're just whores. Right?" He put the glasses back on.

"True. True. Just whores." He walked back over and took another drink from the glass, the water now tasting warm. The glass smelled of mildew. "Why don't you go and show her down. That one you were talkin about. Thought about it some. I guess it is her time after all."

The Rider walked out of the saloon as peaceably and calm as he had entered. He brought the brim of his hat down, keeping his eyes from the sun's gaze; hidden unto himself. He wiped the blade on his pants and placed the knife back in its sheathed scabbard next to the small wet bag that hung swinging from his belt. He untied the black horse from its post and steadied himself on the saddle and rode off, leaving behind him dust gathering in the daylight. The air behind him turned a reddened brown as he went, the upturned earth tracing his path like a small vestibule to ruin.

Inside lay the two: bartender and whore. One fallen on the other. Cradling each other. Their eyes wide, looking futilely about them, somehow holy in their tumid gaze. A thickening pool of darkness collected itself outside of their open mouths, gathering and spilling onto the wood, mixing with the liquid from the broken bottles of alcohol. In their quiet and irresolute sleep of death, they looked as if they were trying to scream out in pain, but they were bereft of voice, for they were both without a tongue to call out into that distant world they no longer inhabited. The world they wished to return to but couldn't.

The Rider

I was nine years old when it happened. When I realized what I was. Who I am. It was on one of those days after I had escaped from my shack of a house after my parents had gotten back home all liquored up from the past night. They were fallen asleep there, my father on the porch steps and my mother in her favorite chair. That chair smelled of tobacco and piss every time I went near it, so I kept my distance. Still remember it. I remember a lot about back then. It was my beginnin in that house. My genesis. It all changed that mornin, and it was that night that I began my exodus. I went down to the river as always on that mornin. The water was as blue as the sky. I could see clouds in the river from above me, them reflectin off that clear water. Fish were skirtin the water, breakin it of its slow movement downstream. Little circles navigatin the cool calmness of it. I read some words from the Book of Deuteronomy then. Book of Laws I remember the preacher said once. I remember fallin asleep to the sounds of the river, the water from the North feedin it always with its sustenance, its life blood. And after a while of layin there I opened my eyes and awoke to the brightest of lights I'd ever imagined shinin in my eyes. Brighter than I could ever believe, than I could ever perceive. Today, reflectin back to then, I see that I did not just wake from my slumbered nap on that mornin, no no no, but I awoke then from the coma sleep I had found myself in every day of my life. I had been sleepwalkin through life like a somnambulist all drugged up on sleep. I won't ever forget the intensity of that light: it was a heavenly glow. Blindin. Like the sun, only it didn't hurt to look at it. I would stare at the sun when I was younger, but I always would look away. This light was different. I couldn't look away from it. Didn't want to. I remember blinkin my eyes at it, tryin to see through its glow but I couldn't see anythin. Just blind as I was. Blind as I had been. But then my eyes began adjustin to it and as they did I saw her. First she was a blur, a haze, a fogged ghost to me, a shadow against the bright. She didn't move, but just stood there, arms down at her side. And I stood too. Slow in my speed. I reached my feet and caught my balance, my eyes never leavin the glow, and extended my hand toward her. Tryin to grab hold of her, this celestial thing. I needed to make sense of her, see if she were real. I hoped so. I hoped so. As I reached out to her the brightness that flooded itself around her went away, disappearin like the wind. Like stars durin the daylight leavin their overlookin perch when the sun rises in the sky. I noticed then, as the light left us, that its divine source came from wings attached to her back. They spread apart, white and thin like cotton. The breeze that swept through us ruffled the sheeted feathers, and yet still she stood silent. Peaceful and beautiful, not movin. And for the first time in my life a stranger made me feel easy, just as the surroundin of nature that I kept myself in made me feel. I was peaceful. The pain from the bruises and cuts on my arms and back left my body. And I felt free. I felt one with life and all that was about me. She was clad in a white robe that stretched to the dirty ground. Brown hair swirlin about in the breeze, this way and that, all directions of the compass, coverin her face, then movin away from it. The swayin locks covered her eyes like she had somethin to hide. Her figure maybe. There still was some kind of rayed brightness about her, comin from both her robe and the wings that seemed at the same time part of and apart from her body. On the robe, though, stainin it's unadulterous white were smeared slashes of red seemin to drip down like muddied liquid from slits. As I stood watchin her, the red bloodied smears grew and spread, like she was bleedin from under the robe outward. The smears grew and spread until they were drippin in a small pool in front of her covered feet. Her hair still moved in the air, the celestial wings that framed her body were still there, still together. She stood like a part of nature, a mute bein that I somehow knew, and she was perfect. But I wanted her to move. It was no dream, I told myself. But I wanted her to move so that I knew she was real. I wanted her to move so I knew this was all happenin. I wanted her to move. I took a step forward, my arm still stretched out, my fingers shakin in fear that she may vanish. And then, finally, I heard her speak to me, yet her mouth did not move. She remained still, her body erect, rigid—like death. But still I felt comfort. Her voice sounded like a whisper in my head. Faint, voiceless. And it said, 'You are more than you know. You are a key to the salvation for all men. You read the Bible and do not realize your place within its pages. It is God's word. And it is your word, as well. The deliverance of man rests upon your shoulders. You lay the road for which man can either walk or stray from. If they walk upon that road with you, they will be saved, if they drift from it, they will be removed, just as man was once removed from Eden. And man is still removed from its gates. You must open that door to mankind and allow him to enter the kingdom.' I stood. I was silent. I didn't know the words she was sayin, but somehow I knew what she was tellin me. I understood it. Those words became imprinted on my memory. I still dream of them, hearin them when I close my eyes, hearin them as I see the gatherin of the multitudes about me, the world surroundin me, beggin me to help them, to lead them to their savior. I dropped my head then on that mornin all those years ago. And the voice of the angel of the Lord said, 'Your path will not be easy. You will be tempted and sacrifices must be made. The rivers will run red with the blood of the wicked. The blood you must spill. It is you who must punish those living in sin. It is your judgment upon them.' And I lifted my head to look at her again, and she moved, slowly, raisin her arms, her hands stretchin upward, palms out to me, and I saw them. Those white hands were covered in the same red liquid as was on her robe. Blood, life, all of it drippin down onto the ground, cuttin through the dust and dirt of the earthly floor and poolin and runnin toward me. She lowered her arms to her sides again and I saw the blood still drippin from the tips of her fingers, still drippin from the tips of her fingers, and the voice said to me, 'Through you, the souls of the just will be saved from damnation. They will be returned once more to the gates from which they were cast away from. It is you, the holy guide, who allows for this.' And then I woke. I opened my eyes and she was gone. I climbed to my feet, brushin the sweat from my face, pantin hard like a dog in the heat of summer and walked over to where she had stood in that dream. And it was not a dream, I told myself over and over. It was not a dream. And I saw it then. There, on the ground, buried under a thin coverin of dust was a pool of blood, still warm and sticky to the touch.

3

Running through a yellowing field of grass and tall grains is a wooden fence. Its pieces are rotting from disrepair and neglect; it seems as if no one has tended to it for years countless, and indeed this is the case. Some of the crossbeams are fallen to the floor and the grass grows over them and buries the wooden pieces, returning them to the earth. The nails have rusted the color of copper black and a putrid shade of green, but you cannot see them on the ground. They have disappeared into the earth, and they will not to be found until years from this time. A young pair, brother and sister, will one day look down to the ground and pull from it these rotted metal pins; they will study the nails, hold them high into the air, and then they will cast them off, allowing the nails to once again become lost in the soil along with the bones and bloodied things buried in time.

In other places along the fence the wild grass climbs up the vertical bars, encircling the wood now in a new coat that is not paint but is natural and yellow and green and orange. And from a distance this wooden fence that once severed this field in two is erased now and it looks of some natural growth that should be there. To some eyes it might even look hidden, its presence erased and all that there is is this field that is now a changing color and dying slowly; but come the rains of the next season it will grow once more green and fresh and new. And eventually, in some unknown time, this fence will be lost forever and the grass and the trees will be all that is left and the fence will be nothing but a palimpsest in this world.

It was late afternoon when he opened the door to the house. The sun was just finishing its disappearance over the rolling hills and jagged treetops along the horizon, a faint incandescence still playing along the ridges. Behind him, coming from the direction of the stable, walked Maria, her head down. Corvin watched each careful step she took—her body a mere silhouette of a being in the setting day. A phantom in the cooling air.

The smell from the kitchen seemed to escape from the house to where he stood, his nostrils invaded with the scent of cooking meat and vegetables from the garden steaming in a pot over the oven fire. The aroma brought his mind back to when he was a boy. He remembered his mother sitting at the table, her back stiff against the high wooden chair as the slave women brought out metal plates and polished trays. She would always look over at him and smile and then bow her head gently in prayer. His father was never in these memories.

He stomped the dirt from his boots on the porch, a black rim coagulated around the soled heel and toe of each shoe, stains from the coal. Maria walked up the stairs of the porch, her tiny shoed feet tenderly tapping the wooden steps, and she joined him. "So," he asked, holding her small hand in his. "What'd you think?"

"Well." She smiled.

He bent low, grabbing hold of her by the waist and brought her close to him and placed his lips to her forehead. She brought her hand up and brushed it along the smooth skin of his cheek, outlining it in her mind, her eyes closed. He brought her head to his chest and held the back of her head, his fingers moving through her hair. Secure and tender. She could hear his heart beating rhythmically and calm. And hers.

"Hungry?" he asked, quietly.

She nodded and they walked inside together, the door shutting softly behind them.

A thin coyote scurries across the narrow road from a gathering of bushes and stops for only a moment to look at the boy perched atop the white horse. Studying him. Each one the other's double. In the coyote's mouth dangles the carcass of a small animal, a bloody pulp from the closed teeth of the predator, and then, as if something beyond the boy startles the animal, it darts away into the setting night. The boy watches the animal go until he can no longer see it. And then the boy rides on.

He looked at her across the table. The candle's flame lit her face, illuminating it within the darkness that surrounded them, consuming the room and world in which they lived. He stretched his hand out across the cloth of the table, and she did the same. Their fingers locked securely within the other's hold.

From the east, the morning sun cast the entire horizon into a vague empyreal glow, a rouge of yellows and reds and oranges that seemed to bleed from the deep blues and purples of the sky. Colors guided from the hollows of the night. The foreshadowed existence of the light swept through the valley. The trees, still nestled in the darkness, seemed to be sleeping quietly. And in some way you would think that these trees did not want the sun's grand light to shine on them and awaken them, or the rest of the world, from their peaceful sleep; for it is only when man has turned his back in sleep that that world is truly allowed to live and grow, reverting again to some ancient time when the earth was dark in the void and there was nothing. It is in that immeasurable time when sleep pervades man and his eyes close that nature begins its chanted prayers for man, sung in the moving air and carried off with the breeze—a silent petition that he may awaken with some newly discovered understanding of that which surrounds and sustains him. Yet man does not seem to hear. He is asleep and he is dreaming. Instead, the light of morning brings about those who forget and have forgotten. Nature itself sings the psalms of memory that it alone can recall; the world simply hears the echoes of what could have been, ringing softly off the mountain sides and along the grassy plains and desert floors, in the river currents.

The Rider pulled back on the reins and the black horse stopped. His breath was visible in the morning air. He looked to the eastern sky and watched the sun's ascent. The shadowed lands before him gained a palatial vibrancy that had existed unseen within the darkness' keep.

He raised his eyes upward and stretched out his arms, embracing the morning air; the myriad stars were losing their glint in the oncoming light, becoming only chimeras in a land of reality. He reached to his side and took his gun from its black leather holster and aimed it at the climbing sun, his arm stretched far in front of him. He cocked the hammer of the gun back with his thumb and pulled the trigger. The sound rang through the valley floor as far as he could imagine and then died out. And everything was silent, just as it had been. He replaced the gun back at his side and began to ride forward at a steady pace, his eyes fixed upon the horizon before him. He watched the land become bright and life sprang from the night's quiet like an orchestra that his eyes seemed to conduct with gleaming precision. The horse's heavy steps awakened dust and powder from the earth that floated about momentarily only to return back to the ground.

Josiah came upon the old man in the early morning. He had ridden through the night without stop and was shivering from the cold. The old man was lying in the open road, prostrate, his lips touching the cool blackness of the earth, his arms extended above him, flat out, his legs in similar fashion below. The boy slowed the horse to a walk when he saw the heap of the man and, after coming closer, he reined the animal to a stop and got off his high saddled mount and patted the horse gently on the snout and walked, stiff and aching, over to the body of the old man and looked down at him.

The clothes of the old man were tattered and frayed, torn into long strips in some places. The once dark blue of his shirt had faded to a white and specks of dried brush and excrement stained it. The pants were a light brown canvas material—holes from moths or time or both lined the legs of them. Spots of dusty white skin showed through. His hair was long and straggled and gray with white streaks and black. It matted to the old man's neck and spilled out onto the soft dirt. He didn't move. Neither one moved.

The boy looked to the horse, seeing that it was wearily walking around, eating some yellowing grass from the bases of the trees. The branches above the three of them—man, boy, and horse—were skeletal and bare, and the ground below them was scattered leaves that clung to the moist soil. Josiah looked back to the haggard form at his feet. After several seconds of watching the old man, the boy kicked the lump and a low muffled grunt escaped it and the old man lifted his head; black mud was clinging to his cheeks and forehead, his eyes were darting wildly, and his mouth was twitching behind a beard and moustache, gray and long and dirty.

Josiah took a step back and watched the old man brush the earthen mask from his wrinkled face and stand. He looked at the boy. "You thirsty?" His voice was rough, as if he hadn't used it in years uncounted.

"Yes," Josiah answered, quietly.

"Hungry?"

"Yes."

"Come along then."

The old man led the boy along the path and they cut through a covering of yellow and brown bushes. The horse followed behind the two, and they walked endlessly through trees and shrubs, the stick fingered branches and prickles cutting into the boy's bare arms. Red scratches traced his skin, blood seeped in places where the branches had dug deep. It itched and the boy scratched. The old man kept walking, not minding the tight fit, not looking back. "Don't scratch it," the old man called behind him, without turning. The boy stopped. The horse circled about in the labyrinthine maze of plants and slowly and methodically made its way behind the leaders.

"Much further?"

The man didn't reply, only kept walking.

The sun was almost to its uppermost place in the sky when a small wooden hut appeared in the distance ahead. It was lodged between a grouping of pines; needles littered the floor surrounding it. When Josiah got closer to the place, he could see that it was of wretched construct, seemingly held together by sheer will of force than by nature's law. A dried and thick mud coated the outer walls in places. Vines yellow and green and blood red in the sun's reflection clung like leeches to other parts of the hut's outside. The small place was low in level. There was a cross beam of blackened wood that ran along the frame of the opened door and the old man had to duck nearly in full to go under it. Along the beam, written in white chalk, were the words "Sola Fide," etched in the wood and fading.

The old man disappeared inside the hut while the boy stayed in the clearing outside, tending to the horse. He walked to the rear of the animal and ran his hand along the leather of the saddle. It was cracked and dried and sharp in places where the tanned skin had curled up and hardened in the cold air and wetness it had endured in the recent days. The horse looked back at him and the boy returned its gaze until he saw the old man coming out from the hut.

"There's a spring in the back out that way." The old man nodded the direction with his head. "Feel free. The both of yeh."

The boy looked over to where the man had motioned and walked to the horse's head and grabbed hold of the reins.

"Mind yer eyes out there," the old man said. He looked up at the boy, seemingly staring through him. And then he continued: "I ain't responsible fer whatever yeh see. Remember that. Ain't my doin. Ain't mine."

The boy nodded and led the horse off and the man watched the two go, around the corner of the shack, slowly and surefooted, and disappearing from his sight.

Behind the hut lay a small garden, a two foot high wooden block ran its perimeter and inside sat a rabbit, quickly chewing away at what was left of the greenery. Weeds of varying colors and lengths surrounded the animal in its supper. Josiah looked at it and continued on. He could hear the faint trickled sound of water, faint in the noon, faint, faint. He continued, the horse behind him. As they breached the trees fencing the small hovel from the forest about, a smell wafted through the air. It was sweet and crisp, wretched and abused all at once. The boy looked around, searching for the cause of the scent that smelled indistinct and absurd in the reality of the world. The horse shied and stamped its feet hard, jerking its head back in some ominous foretelling.

Beyond a close thicket of trees, clustered together—their ennobled bases standing erect—ran a thin stream that collected itself into a small pool. Water bubbled and surged forth here. And, as they approached the water, the smell grew stronger and more. The horse dropped its head and lapped from the stream, the sound repetitive and harmonious with the buzzing of fly's wings and the steady chirps of crickets off in the unnamed forest about. The boy took off his worn and musty hat and dropped to his knees, sticking his face deep into the cold water. It stung his face. He drank along with the horse, swallowing the same spring water from the small stream as those unnumbered before him. When he lifted his head, black water and soot and dirt streaked down his face. He wiped the dripping liquid from his lips with the back of his hand and drank two handfuls more. He looked back, toward the hut; the old man was nowhere in sight, yet the boy could feel his eyes watching. The horse continued drinking and the boy turned to it, watching the water fall from the animal's tongue back to the earth from whence it came. The boy looked out beyond the stream's reach, out to the trees and groves you couldn't see save for your imagination. He moved his gaze farther downstream. And that's when he saw them.

Some seven feet above the ground, stretching between the remnants of two trees—downed and spliced by some primeval storm—was a long wood beam eight or nine feet in length. The splintered thing was latched with rope and driven through with nails and it was reinforced in areas along its reach with other pieces of wood that were nailed together. It sagged downward with the weight that it carried; some modern and satanic albatross was its anchor. Along the length of the beam were five black bodies hanging upside-down in an ungodly position. They were each of them held by the skin and bone of their ankles; the beam cut through and held them each captive in some chain gang from which there was no longer a hope of freedom or escape. An unsteady and hating crucifix of unknown terror and existence. The bigger ones' hands had scratched the dirt beneath, leaving trailed circles in the powder and dust.

They were rotting and the flesh was ripped off in pieces from where buzzards and other scurrying animals had feasted. They seemed to be floating in midair, motionless. The breeze blew all about, even within the shade of the trees, yet they remained still.

Josiah stood and picked up his hat from where it rested and walked to where the bodies were, splashing through the spring, feeling the crisp sting of the water on his blackened feet. He stood before them and watched, suspecting movement, waiting for some flinch or twitch that never came. He studied each, examining the faces. Two men, a woman, a small girl of five or six, and a newborn not a year old; each was naked save the minimal clothing of skin that each still owned.

The boy reached a hand out slowly and touched it against the cold skin of one of the larger bodies. It was damp and like a fish's skin and felt as if it could peel off if he rubbed any harder. He stopped and wiped his hand on his pants and turned around toward the hut. The old man was nowhere in sight. The horse was still drinking from the stream when Josiah patted the animal's flank and led it back through the grove from where they had come, leaving the trees and their ghoulish inhabitants behind. He didn't look back.

The old man was crouched on the ground drawing circles in the mud with his finger when Josiah led the horse back. The horse was gaunt and weak, its skeletal ribs pushing out, showing each anatomical movement it made through its skin. The boy, too, looked emaciated—the long coat and baggy denims, his face shrunken and deep, his cheek bones high and sharp now. The boy tethered the horse's leather strap to a tree's branch and looked down at the figure before him. "Thank you for the water."

The old man nodded his head rightly at the boy and then dropped his gaze back to the dirt, muttering some chanted whisper of thanks or apologies to the earth. Then he stood. "Ain't mine to give, but yer welcome." The old man's eyes held a childlike sadness, a quiet innocence in the dulled and clouding corneas. His fingers twitched back and forth as he stood and he wiped them on the front of his shirt, leaving a trail of black and brown dirt. Then he flipped his head to the side, getting a long and straggled grouping of hair from out of his face, and, with an abrupt turn, walked into the house again. The boy followed, ducking low under the Sola Fide beam and into the shack.

It was dark and smelled of urine inside. No candle flicker illuminated the walls, no window was there to allow the sun's light to invade the room; the only light came from the front opening from which they had just walked through. Josiah turned and looked closer at the front opening now. There was no door—he could see that; on the side, attached by nails was a rude sheet of thick canvas with holes and dirt lining its body. It was fastened up into a bunch by another nail and the cloth seemed to drape in the corner shadows of the opening, unsuspected. In the center of the room was a table and a chair. Josiah could make out the faint silhouetted outline of a mass heaped on the table. The passing light from behind him shimmered through the place and he took a step closer to the table. The old man reached down and hauled the mass up and balanced it onto his shoulder and forged past the boy and out into the daylight again. Josiah took one more look into the dark lit room, noticing a small wooden cot with a stack of animal hides and furs for a mattress and blanket in the far right corner. Then he turned and followed the old man out.

"How long you been out?" The old man was seated on the dirt

floor next to where the boy had found him drawing figures in the mud moments before. On the man's lap was the carcass of a fox, gray and orange and black, its head missing. The man's shirt and pants were stained with the newly dead animal's blood

"A bit over a week now, I reckon." The boy sat.

"Hmm." The old man pushed the dead animal's body off him and stood and walked back into the shack and came back out quickly and sat. In his hands he held two plates; balanced on top of the plates was a rusting knife and a dead bird. The plates were terra-cotta, worn and reminiscent of ancient native sculptings; the bird was long and slender and half of its feathers were missing. Its head was turned back, facing the opposite direction. The old man set the dirty knife and the bird on the ground next to him and handed the boy a plate. It was red and grainy. The boy took it and looked at it closely, rubbing his hand over the texture.

"Found these long time ago," the old man said. "Mexicans made em. Down on the Texas border. Some forty years gone by now I suppose. Was jus settin there. Still warm with food. Others, they took em and threw em in the air, shootin em down like they was targets. Not me, though. No sir. I put these two and a bowl in my bag. Still servin me good still."

The boy nodded.

"Sent us down there to slay them savages. They called em that. Most was more civil than us, though. Still today it's such. Them that're left that is." The old man looked at his hands and rubbed them over each other. He talked to the ground, as if the boy were not there and he was reciting a speech he had given often before: "We went down there and slay whole villages, no matter what they was: man, woman, child, armed, not, old. No matter." He looked up at the boy now. "I done many a things I ain't proud of, seen more things I can't never fancy humans havin the capacity of evil to do. But, then again, I remind myself ever now and then that evil can wear the face of an angel too." He paused and picked up the bird and looked at it a while. "I been tryin to clear my mind of that, cleanse my conscience. My soul. Ain't nothin worked, though. Ain't God nor man can make a person forget the things they done. Or regret."

The old man picked up the knife at his side and dug it deep into the bird and scraped it down the bony, thin chest. He separated the small chest bone with his fingers and pulled the tiny cage of it out. He brought the red bone to his mouth and began to pick away the stringy muscle still attached, chewing the meat and spitting a frothy red liquid next to him on the dirt. He handed the bird across to the boy and then began to cut into the hide of the fox. He sliced open the animal at its underside and continued cutting around the body, stripping the red pelt from the animal in one long and consecutive piece.

Josiah looked down at the bloody pulp in his hands and looked back to the man before him, who was hard at work, using the large knife in a sawing motion. Blood covered the man's shirt and pants, spraying in small spurts out of the animal, but the old man didn't seem to notice. The boy set the bird down next to him and watched his companion. Josiah looked to his horse and saw the animal munching on some grass near the base of the tree he was tied to. The horse gazed up at the boy and then dropped its head down and went back to eating.

The old man was just finishing with the hide of the fox, laying the crimson sheet out between the two of them. "I'll have to go wash this up a bit." He sliced off a thin layer of meat from the dead animal and began to chew it raw. Blood stained his mouth and lips and the tip of his nose and he wiped his face with the back of his hand and continued. He made a loud smacking sound with each chew. He spat again. "Caught these not a hour afore I seen yeh in the road," he said, not looking up but continuing to eat.

Josiah nodded quietly.

The old man smiled and handed the knife across to the boy and pushed the stripped animal forward. Josiah took the knife wearily. The man smiled again. "When yeh live without fire and learn to eat only when yer stomach gives yeh cramps to notice, yeh don't mind what it is it looks like or what it tastes like for that matter. An I figure there ain't much point in tryin to act like we ain't animals. It's what we are, ain't it? Ain't no sense denyin it." He chewed and swallowed a piece. "The taste wears on yeh though and after a long enough while yeh don't care to have a cooked meal or not."

The boy sliced a thin piece of meat off the bloody thing and chewed it. It was juicy and tasted of metal and it smelled wretched, but the boy kept chewing and swallowed the lump of meat and cut off another sliver and digested that too.

After they had had their fill of meat, the two sat back on their hands and stretched their legs out before them. "You see em out back there?" The old man sat up straight and began to pick the grime from beneath his long and yellowing fingernails.

"Yeah."

"Ain't me."

"You said that."

"I know. It ain't, though." The old man brought his fingers up to his mouth and bit off one of his nails and spat it out into the distance. "Death and hate son. All life is. There is some good, though. Yeh look hard nuff an ye'll find some decency out there. I promise yeh that, son. Ain't much of it, but it's there. Hard to find." He took a deep breath and then exhaled slowly. "Seems I been tryin to run from it; jus keeps follerin me. Think after some time God'd jus let me be, but then I go out to drink some someday not long back an see em jus hangin there. Never saw who it was. Ain't me, though. Guess it's jus my punishment of fightin a war I never wanted to. One I never unnerstood. Yeh gotta believe in what yeh do, son. Believe in yer life. It's yers to decide. Yer choices."

The boy was quiet. He sat up and crossed his legs, running his hands over his pants.

"Killed lot of people. Some innocent. Can't never forget them. See the faces always. See them in my dreams at night. See them when I look at my face in the water. Bloody and cryin, holdin out their hands to me like I could save em. I never did, though." He shook his head slowly from side to side. "Never can go back and change it. No. Yer consequences lay with yeh. Always. Follers yeh. I reckon all people in this world jus tryin to keep livin an unnerstandin theyselves best they can, live with the choices they made. But I'll tell yeh, son. Yer choices haunt yeh til there ain't much left to think about, til there ain't much left to do cept ask God fer some repentance, kindness, or a showin at least that he still cares. Hopin he hears me. Don't really know if he does, though. But I try."

"That what you were doin in the road out there?"

The old man nodded. "Always supposed if roads were for travelin then maybe some day I'd meet him, or someone else that can show me where I'm to look." The old man was silent; he looked away, back toward the stream behind the hut and then he returned his gaze on the boy. "You ain't him, is yeh?"

"No." Josiah shook his head. "Don't reckon."

"Could be."

"I ain't." He picked up a bone from the massacred cartilage beside him and looked at the stringed tendons wisping about.

The old man held the boy in his gaze and smiled slightly. He reached out and turned the fox skin between them over at the flap and began to run his blackened fingers along the soft coat. "Why you out here, boy?"

"Searchin."

"Fer what."

Josiah gave no answer. He quietly thought of the question. He wasn't entirely sure if he knew what to say.

"You an orphan, boy."

"Am now."

"What happened?"

"Don't matter none."

The old man nodded his head and picked at the spaces between his yellow and chipped teeth with one of his long, slender fingernails.

After a while the boy said, "You seen a man on horse come

through this way?"

"He what yer searchin?"

"Maybe. Not really sure."

The old man stood and stretched his arms high above him, reaching up towards the tops of the shading trees and further up still to where light becomes dark and answers are void and forgotten. He brought them back down, letting his fingers nervously twitch again. "Naw, son. Can't say I have, an I'm sorry fer that." He shook his head. "Yer the first livin civilized soul I seen round here in a while. Cept fer those negroes out there there ain't no one else cept me been out here that I could tell yeh. Usually I like it alone. Always have. Solidarity and quietness. Hand in hand. Ain't solitude that I'm seekin, though, mind you. I ain't tryin to live a peaceful life out here. Them ghosts keep watch over that, an they keep me right. I start to settle down a bit and lose my mindfulness on the past an they wake me and scream at me to wake and then I do and then I lay awake and hear the animals out past the walls of my place here and wonder in the back of my mind if it ain't them ghosts comin to seek their vengeance. To tell yeh, most nights I hope it is them comin fer me. Ain't never seen em, but I know they're there." His eyes wandered about the small clearing to the trees surrounding them, as if he were searching for someone that was watching them. He stood and reached down and took the hide from the ground and hung it over a renegade branch that was jutting out from the base of one of the nearby trees. An old worn shirt hung next to it. He turned and faced the boy. "What's this man on horse look like?"

"Can't tell much. He's ridin a big black horse. Looked dressed in black. I couldn't nearly see him when I did."

The old man looked off past the boy to the stream, off to where the bodies dangled in unison. He seemed to be reflecting on the very existence of him or the boy or both. He spoke quietly, as if to himself. "I seen the rider in black. Some times I would look out past the carnage about me, past my friends and my enemies and I'd catch a quick glance at him. Alone and quiet on his dark steed. I only truly seen him once though." He looked to the boy, a faint glimmer of a tear staining the undercurrents of his eyes, "Yer chasin Death, boy. You unnerstand that?"

The boy looked up and shook his head. "No, sir. He's man enough. Only man can do what he done. I seen it."

The old man sat down again, thudding to the ground heavily, defeated. "Back then, in the war with them Mexicans, we'd ride the whole of us until we found some village and we'd go in and kill everthin. Take the women and have them and then kill em when we were done. After we left, the dirty streets would all be covered in blood—blood so thick it'd cling to yer boots, smell stay with yeh fer days, stain yer skin—but we never minded it none. Never thought much bout what we did then. We all thought it right, I reckon. They told us we was exterminatin evil from the world, one non-Christian after next. That's what they said when I joined. Told me I could be a savior, a warrior fer good. And be rich. And I bought it all, believed it all.

"I can recount each of their faces. Each woman I took then shot—the feel of her unner me, squirmin this way an that, fightin with me the whole while—an I can see the faces of each child I stabbed and bled out, each elder person I broke and dragged." He was quiet. He continued after a while: "We'd heap em all in the town center when we were done and burn em all. The smoke'd be nigh as tall as the birds flew and wider'n the town. Jus floatin up. Dark as night, boy. Dark as night. And smellin like sulfur and metal and shit and piss all. Burnin hair, too. I can still smell it. And the lot of us standin about jus drinkin and laughin and carryin on with smiles on our faces and gold in our bags. We'd laugh like nothing happened.

"In the mornin some'd be asleep drunk on the streets, them jus lyin there. The blaze would jus be settlin down but the smoke'd still be stretchin up to God. An we'd all wake and move on to the next town and then the next, and that's how it was then.

"But on them nights we traveled it'd be cold and I'd cling down to my horse to feel some warmth I could, an I'd tuck my blanket about me, wearin the coats of some dead Mexican I killed. And I'd look out cross the desert an that's when I'd see him walkin along on his mount. Always looked dark and blendin into the night, but by the moon I could see him clear. Never knew who he was. Shit, son, I can't tell yeh if he was truly there, but I would always see him there. Always there at night. Always walkin alongside us in the distance, like he was watchin us. It always felt like he was watchin me, to tell yeh the truth. I always figured he was jus some mirage then, some ghost in the night. But it wasn't til I met the General that I unnerstood who that rider was."

The old man stood again and walked over to the hut and went in. Josiah followed him with his eyes, watching as the man's head bent low beneath the Sola Fide beam. The old man emerged from the hut seconds later carrying a small bag of water made from the innards of some animal. The man sat back down and handed the loose makeshift canteen over to the boy. Josiah took a couple gulps of the warm water and handed it back, his eyes never leaving the man. The old man took it back and drank the rest of what was left and then set the bag down on the ground. A bird called in the distance. It was answered by another, then another. The two sat quietly, though.

Josiah wiped his mouth with the back of his hand. "Who was the General?" His voice sounded weak and tired.

The old man looked up quickly, as if surprised by the boy's words, and then shook his head. He cleared his throat. "Never knew his real name. Probably wasn't no general neither, but that's what they all called him and I jus followed suit, I suppose. Anyways, we come cross him down there near the western border of Texas, right there where they tell yeh that Mexico starts. Him and his men jus walkin round killin whatever, jus like us, usin whatever and takin whatever, jus like us, but there was somethin different with him. I tell yeh, I seen it the first time I laid eyes on him. Wasn't a big man by no means, kinda meek and scrawny, but he made up for that.

"We come up, stragglin about, jus tryin to find some water

out there. Sand surroundin yeh. Hot as can be, boy. An out in the distance some mile or such from where we was, we seen this big heap of smoke come raisin up from the horizon, like we'd circled back to one of em towns we'd jus been from. Lookin familiar to all us. Jus bigger—a lot bigger. So we come up on this town near night break an see the smoke still blowin up to the sky, seemed like Revelations was comin true that day, sky black, an the sun an moon burnin a blood red. We come up, our weapons drawn like we was prepared for some battle, some fight we ain't never known before. An we see, in the streets, white men with our colored shirts ridin about an walkin about, none of em drinkin or such like we was when we'd taken a town. No. They was gatherin all them things they could find and heapin em in the blaze an goin back fer more. Men goin into huts and bringin out blankets an clothes, baskets, furs, everthin and jus throwin them in that fire and walkin back for more.

"We asked one of them boys walkin out of a hut with belongins, askin him what they was doin an he jus said they was cleanin the town. Cleansin it— may have been what he said. Can't recall completely. An we ask him who was in charge an he jus nods off toward the fire blaze and says only, 'the General' an carries on as if we was never there. Didn't ask who we was, nothin. So we go over to where the boy nodded off to, circlin about the fire, keepin distance from the heat that was jumpin out at us, our little rackety troop, an we find this man standin nearly in the fire. All we see is his body outlined in the flames, I remember it—his hands were upstretched an in one of his hands he was holdin a giant military sword that looked to be on fire from the flames in front of him, an his hands were swingin back an forth liken he was conductin them flames. Seemed like he was waitin fer us, or someone else, an he jus happened to find us instead.

"He met and shook hands with our captain. An our captain explained to this man who we was and what we did and then this General walks over to us and smiles and seemed to look into each of us, his eyes, my God, and he says to us that we was doin a higher powered biddin than we knew. He said that killin was the way to savin an that we was all workin good fer what we believe, that we was all savin lives, even if we didn't know it. I never unnerstood much what he said, maybe not much to unnerstand, maybe too much. I'm not sure. He told us then that he was the General an that we could trust him and that we should get some water an food an rest cuz in the mornin, I remember his words here, said in the morning we was 'to see the power of man an the power that God gave man an the beauty of death.'

"An so I wake next mornin an see the sun peekin out over cross the dusty nothin that stretched ever which way I could see. I stood and looked about me an saw a couple more of my group men still sleepin. Off, not far, the fire was still burnin bright as the General's men was tearin down the huts and throwin the wood an mud an straw an sand all into the inferno. They walked as if they had no purpose but to carry loads and throw into the fire again an again. Seemed machines or such. Couldn't unnerstand it. I walked in the direction of the fire an saw the General. He was standin as tall an erect as a man could, smilin into the flames, watchin them destroy everthin they touched. I walk up an said a good mornin to him and noted his skinny face, looked like he'd been starved for weeks. His nose was long and his face was a deep red, an one thing I ain't never gonna forget is the huge bushy moustache he had. Seemed to circle down from his lips down to his neck, big like I ain't never seen. An although it was morning, me an everone else I saw was sweatin an sweatin, but I didn't see one drop of sweat or wetness on him at all. An I looked down at his right hand, notin how it was stained a deep red, the skin raw like it been burned away an scarred over by a fire or some such thing. Horrid sight. Still see it when I shut my eyes.

"He said good mornin an asked that I follow him. Told me he wanted to show me something, and then he turned and started to walk off past his men, past where I had slept an where the others still did, walkin off into some separate part of the town I didn't care to know of. I followed behind him, though. I stayed quiet an still in amaze at the men carryin the wood, them quiet and with a kind of devotion, as if penance were what they were after.

"I stepped over my sleepin partners and off behind them, an I hid in his shadow until he stopped an I come up beside him an I stop too an I look down at his feet where he's lookin an I see lyin there in the dust the figure of my captain, the man I had seen naught the night before lead us into that town. I stooped down to look closer; I couldn't believe it was him, didn't think it was, couldn't tell. What rested before me was nothin but a heap of skin smeared with blood that circled about it. Deep blade cuts an slices ran the length of the arms an legs an throat area. The head of this thing was twisted completely backwards, its arms sprawled out reachin for somethin it couldn't get to. But I remember how there was not a bit of blood on the ground where he was layin at. An I stood an looked back from where I walked an then I looked over to the General. He said it was the work of one of the escaped villagers. Then, without sayin nothin else, he turns an walked away. I stared back at what was once my captain and leader an then followed the General again, this time his shadow slanted farther off to the west, and I watch it move along the red an brown dirt.

"I followed him back an we come up to a place where all I could see was bodies heaped upon another, all of them face down on the ground. An there was the smell of rot that came up to my nose. Almost gagged and had to spit some to try to take the taste of death from off my tongue. An I seen them all then. There was five separate piles if I reckon correct, bout twenty or thirty bodies to each. One was old men, one was old women, one was a mix of kids not ten years aged with some dogs gathered in too, one was men, an the last was women. Them corpses looked ragged as sheets an light too, like they would blow off with the smallest wind.

"We walked past the stinkin bodies that were all collectin bunches of birds peckin at the dryin skin—I could hear the steady chompin of those beaks eatin away at the skin—an I could hear the hummin of the damned bugs, and see em too, thick as storm clouds movin about before us, jus over them bunches of bodies. But we jus kept walkin, the General leadin an me behind.

"Not a hundred steps past the last of the heaps I began to hear it. Not loud, but there nonetheless. Sounded of bags droppin an scraped along rock an dirt; no voices, none I could hear anyways. An off to the right of the piles was a wall that faced where we was, hidin the noises I could hear. It seemed out of place, like there'd been a house there once but no more, cleared an gone by God or man. An the closer we got to that wall the louder the scrapin got an I could see pools of wet hot blood on the ground streamin around the side of the wall and movin toward me, some river of no name bein created.

"We walked around the wall an I saw them: lined up, hands tied an bound behind their backs, leather straps tied about their heads, bundles of leather in their mouths like animals, keepin em from talkin a peep. Some of em were cut an bleedin, all of em were dirty an scarred, faces already white with death. An they all jus stood, waitin to die.

"Runnin along the bottom of the wall was ten or twelve dead bodies that were bein drug away by some of the General's men, past us an to the body piles. As the bodies were cleared from the wall, those in line were led, five or so at a time, a mix of man, woman, an child, an they was pushed back against the wall an told to close their eyes. 'Shut yer eyes!' they say, '*Cierra los ojos*.' Then, three of the General's men would walk to them people an slow like, with long knives, would slice each of the prisoner's throats. Some would spit blood, others would jus fall an then they would stay there, their bodies jerkin this way an that some, their blood addin to the river, givin it its power to keep runnin. An then another five were told to go an see their own death with their eyes closed. 'Don't wanna waste no bullets on these niggers. Save em bullets fer killin somethin worth em,' he said to me. 'It's destiny,' he said, 'Ours to conquer, theirs to die.'

"I stood alone, watchin as the General's men drug the bodies away, watched the blood scrape in lines, the feet all cut up bein taken away an stacked up an I looked back to the General but he wasn't next to me no more. He was off at the line of those villagers waitin their turn to the wall an I see him talkin to one of the men in the lines, an then the man spat in the General's face an what I saw next I ain't never forgot, probably never will. I see the General wipe his face an then he leans in an sinks his teeth onto the man's nose an with a jerk of his head, the man fell an landed on his back screamin out, an the General spat the man's nose at him an then pulled out his revolver an shot the man in the head. He bit that thing clean off an then he walked back over to where I stood. I in unbelief. An he had blood all round his mouth an spat some bloody spit out onto the dirt beside us. 'Can't save all the bullets,' he says, and then wipes his face with his hand, gettin all that blood an gore from out his moustache and off his lips an cheeks.

"I looked into his eyes, boy, an what I seen I know wasn't man. It was darker, more evil. An I asked him then how I could trust him that he didn't kill my captain after the thing I jus seen him do an all he says to me, as he wiped the spit from his lips, was '*Sola Fide.*'

"I turned then an ran to my horse where I had him restin next to the water well not far from the burnin pile an I rode out as fast as I could.

"I rode through that night, nearly fallin from the saddle in tired and disgust, scared of that thing of a man, seein him an those ghosts come chasin me in my mind. An out there on the edge of ground an sky, ain't but a little distance away, I saw a single rider in black an behind him a line of people stretchin as far back as I could believe, jus walkin. It looked like some holy exodus. An I turned my horse from them people an rode as fast I could, don't really know why but I did. I stopped after a few paces an watched them. On the horse was a shadow rider, the animal like the night save its eyes, and I knew it was death an he was watchin me as he rode an I was scared an hopin at the same that he might take me with him after the things I knew an seen an the things I done, but he kept goin along. An I watched those people followin him, mostly Mexican it looked, like the people from the piles I had jus come from that day; they was walkin slowly, some smilin an others cryin it seemed, an there in the back somewhere I swear I could see my captain lookin out in the dark, pleadin me to help or do somethin or join him, but instead I jus turned again an rode away an left em to go wherever it was they was headed."

Josiah had remained attentively silent and thoughtful throughout the man's story. Occasionally, he would rub his eyes or look off into the distance, around him, run his fingers through the hard grain of the dirt beneath him, trying in some way to accept the truths of that which he couldn't believe and the falsities of that which he knew were real.

In the old man's eyes there was a collection of tears that ran halfway down his cheek before he wiped them away and looked at the boy. "I've sat many days of my life replayin it all in my head. Can't never make no sense of it; all I know's I was caught in the middle of somethin bigger than me an that's all. You're the first person I ever told it to. Still don't make it none easier fer me. Jus as confusin as the day it happened. I guess the only way that any of it makes sense, that whole part of my life, was to unnerstand it through faith, an believe in that faith. Faith—I keep that with me as a reminder all throughout, got it carved in an written up there. Don't know if yeh saw it there or not before. *Sola Fide.*" He pointed over to the cross beam; the boy followed with his eyes. The old man cleared his throat with a cough and began again: "Son, yer chasin right after death hisself. Let me tell yeh one thing—If yeh go searchin out death, yer gonna find it, one way or another. But yer gonna have to enter through hell in doin so an the question then is how yeh to end up on the other side. Yeh get in the middle of doin somethin yeh don't have no unnerstandin of an yeh better watch yerself." His fingers began to twitch again, this time stronger and more noticeable. "Death an the devil ain't the same thing, but it is a lot like the devil. Yeh go searchin it out an ye'll find it; thing is though, it might not be what yeh really want."

"Ain't Death I'm searchin. I told yeh, the man I seen and what he done, only man can do that."

"What yeh aim to do then?"

"Ride til I find him."

"An then?"

"I'll know when I see him."

They sat a while, their eyes joined together in searching the dirt between them. Then the man spoke. "Well then, son, yeh jus remember the words I told yeh. I hope that they be a lesson to yeh, but, then again, they was jus a story, me the teller an yeh the ears. Without listenin ears, what power is a teller left with? Huh? Nothin. He's alone then, left with nothin but his own inglorious thoughts; thoughts quieted in the mind before they become beliefs, but once they become them beliefs there ain't no ridden yerself of em. They're stuck with yeh then and you with them til there ain't no decipherin which way truth is an which way doubt or lie or if there's even a difference between them." The old man looked up and began to sniff at the air. "Rain's comin, boy. Yeh wanna stay the night dry, yer welcome to stay here. Don't get no company out here never."

The boy stood and wiped the dust from his pant-legs and stretched his arms out at their sides in a stretch. "I best be gone. I thank yeh for the food and company."

Josiah gathered what little he had with him and unhitched the horse from where he had tied it and began to lead it away into the deep forest. The old raconteur watched the boy walk away, following the two figures until they were almost disappeared from sight, and then the man yelled after the boy, as if in afterthought, "Ain't me killed them negroes. I jus found em that way. Ain't me." In the surrounding of the trees and bushes, the old man's call was merely a hush and he was left alone, musing his place both in the world as it was and as it was not, before and after him, in the living and the dead and the musty coverings in between.

The Rider

I went straight home and hid myself inside my small room, my cave from the other inhabitants of that place. I still had the numbing feeling that tingled all through my skin when I had seen the celestial being. I still couldn't understand what she had told me. In my head I could hear her voice still, as if she were still there callin to me, from inside my head, callin, recitin it to me: 'You are the key to the salvation for all men. Through you, the souls of the just will be saved from damnation. It is you, the holy guide, who allows for this.' I could hear that sweet voice as I shut my eyes that warm afternoon, as I tried to understand the purpose to which she was alludin. And I finally drifted off to sleep, still thinking bout it. Asleep on the floor of my cave. That evenin I awoke as I normally did. The door slammed shut and my parents came into the house screamin and kickin each other, cussin and clawin. I sat up where I still lay, remindin myself of what the angel had told me, still tryin to believe it, to grasp what it was she was tellin me. I had dreamed of her in my sleep. And I picked up the Bible and began to leaf through the pages, hopin for an answer and an escape from my parents in the other room. I drew a blanket up over my body and held it tight to my skin, thinkin that it could hide me from them, that it could protect me. But just as I was turnin the pages, I heard the door open and the thumped thumped bootsteps of my father walkin across the unsteady planked flooring that I was cowerin down upon. My body began to shake. I could hear my breath comin quicker. Louder and quicker. Then he grabbed the blanket and threw it from my skin and stood me up and swiped at me across my face.

I felt the warm sting that I had gotten used to. In my hand I still held the Bible, opened to where I had turned it last. Then he hit me again, this time harder and he almost fell. In the other room I could hear my mother tellin him to leave me be, ain't somethin she did much. And then she come burstin into the room with her half empty bottle of shine and began to beat him across the back of the head with it, connectin once or twice, then she threw the bottle and hit him in the back. He looked back at her, she now cowerin in the corner of the room like a scared animal in a cage. He looked back at me and tried to grab the Bible from my hand. It was still open and I tugged and pulled at it until the book slipped from my hand and I was left with only a single ripped sheet. I clung to it as if it were the last thing I owned in my life. He took the Bible and threw it down on the floor and bent down and picked up the bottle that was now broken on the ground and threw it at me. It hit my arm and cut a gash in it that started to bleed down to my clenched fist with the Bible page. I stood there, ready to take whatever he was about to do, thinkin that the angel would be there to protect me. My father stood there, cussin at me, tellin me I was nothin, a mistake, a joke, an accident, and then he pulled out his knife from where he kept it sheathed on his belt and came walkin toward me, howlin how he was gonna end it, my mother screamin at him to stop and me just standin there ready. The knife was big in his hand. And I remember how the blade shined in the dim light of the room. He slashed at me and sliced my other arm, just above my elbow and still I stood. Then he slashed quick at my face and I was lyin on the ground, my left eye feelin sealed shut, burnin my skull and feelin wet and cold on the skin. Next to my face was the bottle that he'd thrown at me and without givin it thought I stood and swiped at his flailin hand that held the knife. I connected and saw the cut marks and blood on his hand. He screamed out and dropped the knife and bent, doubled over, holdin his hand. I dropped the bottle and then bent down and grabbed the knife from where it lay and ran at him with all my speed and force and jammed the knife into his chest. The two of us fell together on the floor, me on top of him and him gaspin for air and screamin out. Then I took the blade out of him and pressed it back down where his heart was and then out and then back in, over and over, in his chest and then his neck and finally at his face, each time feelin his body tense and jerk and then settle, a small gasp leakin from his lips each time until he didn't move or make a sound and there was nothin but a bloody sack before me. The whole while, my mother had been silent in the corner until I stood above the body of my father with the knife in my hand. It was then that she came rushin at me, screamin and wailin and jumped on me, throwin me to the floor, me under her heavy weight. I felt her body wrench some and her breath grow weak and strained and then I saw her eyelids close gentle and her body slump even heavier now. I pushed her off some and struggled my way out from under her and saw the blade still stuck in her top chest near her neck. I hadn't meant to do it but she had ran into me and ran into the blade and I stood and looked down at my two dead parents. And I smiled. I reached down and pulled the blade from her and kept it closed in my hand. In my other hand I still had the torn page. I wiped the blood from my stingin, burnin face and looked down at the page and read the verse and knew who I was and what the angel meant for me. 'The righteous shall rejoice when he seeith the vengeance: he shall wash his feet in the blood of the wicked.' I stood above my dead wicked parents and was bathed in their blood, and in so doin I was freed of their sins. I walked out the door of the house. In one hand I held the knife and in the other I was pressin a cloth against my bleedin face. And I knew what I was to do. What I was to do. To do. To do. Do.

4

If you were to look out over the distant landscape of this place you would see yourself in the absence, in the void of things. And in so seeing, you would be given chance to view and judge this land and this world as if it were a mirrored reflection of yourself, for if you are one with all, then those other things become you until we spiral out of our control and lose our hold on what is what and who is who, because we are merely all things that have come before us. And nothing more.

The clamoring steps of the horses thudded across the rocky terrain and echoed throughout the still peaceful and frozen valley. The land seemed asleep still in the early morning hours when the sun just begins to stretch its way to the heavens, throwing an incandesced radiance to all the small creatures rising and setting out in the new dawn. The graveled rocks seemed to shatter under each heavy hoof and flick up and settle back with every stride of the animal's flanks and every hushed and fogged snort of the horse's breath seemed to ring out in the heavy dewed air and evaporate within its own stirring.

From where he rode, Corvin could hear Maria's quiet laughter as she rode beyond him. There was no true destination in their ride except to free themselves and each other from the realities of life and the strains of business, which seemed to follow their movements like a shadow that could not be erased, even in the darkness of night. The steady letters and telegrammed messages, the constant flow of workers and their questions. "Coal. Money." He smiled as she turned back to him and yelled breathless in the crisp air: "Catch up."

As they crested one of the many rock strewn slopes, he looked out to the west and noticed some twenty miles away the gathering of darkened storm clouds and he thought he could smell the early drops of rain in the distance. Then he turned back and sunk his spurred heals deep into the horse's sides and felt the animal speed up to meet her.

The Rider stood quiet on the ridge, watching below him the steady line of walking congregants moving in unisoned movement to the water's edge. All were clothed in white sheet, marching forth with their heads bowed in deep contemplation, as if weighing their own lives before themselves, afraid of the very judgment that they each would bring. The Rider was hidden among the trees that stretched down to the calm river, and he became nothing more than an extension of shadow from one of the many reaching arms of these trees.

He looked back behind him. The black horse was chewing on some nearby grass. Peaceful. He looked back to the congregation and knelt on one knee, watching with close interest the many men and women before him. They drew themselves into two separate lines—men and women—just at the edge of the river, where water became land and land became water. Each person stood on the banks in a serene quiet, waiting to stride out to the lone man dressed in black who waded up to his waist in the cold and purifying water. This man held the Bible high over his head, showing it proudly to all around him. He was calling out something in a deep and resonanced tone that The Rider could not hear, save for the scattered fragments of words and sentences and breaths and whispered thoughts.

Each of the members cloaked in white would stride out with heads still bowed and fall back with the guided and gentle hand of the preacher into the water, allowing it to consume their bodies and their souls, letting the water rush over them and drench them in its renewing breath. The black leather Bible the last thing they would see before the water washed all sight away and left them with nothing but resurrection. Their lungs would tighten in the cold of the water and for a flitting second they would lose faith in the man holding them under and give all to something else. And then surface again, gasping for air.

As he watched each white-clad member walk off, drenched and alive, The Rider began to weep. Tears came streaming uncontrolled down his hard cheeks but he did not wipe them away. His eyes remained fixed on each person below him. After some time, The Rider stood and began to walk back to the black horse awaiting his return. His eyes were red and itched. Overhead, the clouds darkened and rain began to fall, stinging his skin and soaking his clothes through. He closed his eyes and looked up to the sky in a moment of rapturous bliss and stretched out his arms to feel the heavy thudded drops caress his body. And he stood still, entrenched in the joy of his own baptismal shower, as if it were a sign from above.

Josiah was not three miles upriver from The Rider. He was looking for some form of shade from the coming deluge of the morning; the sky above was darkened and gray, holding not a drop of sunlight, but rather throwing the entire surrounds in a dullness. Rain drops began to fall to the ground around him. They felt heavy and cold on his skin and he could hear the steady drumming of the falling water on the river, the earth, and the trees above him. Birds became ceased of their noisy calls and all he could hear was the rain.

He walked his horse over to a gathering of trees, the limbs of which stretched out over the water of the river, as if sheltering it from the falling rain. He sat, leaning his back on the tree's base, drawing his dirty overcoat up over his head; in his hands, beneath the coat, he held his rifle, keeping it dry.

After several minutes, Josiah set the rifle down in one of the few dry spots on the ground and stood and walked over to where the horse was. He ran his fingers along the side of the animal's face, feeling the faint twitches of the running blood in the veins, the soft and slow heartbeat, the quiet blink of its eyes.

The place around him smelled, but the boy didn't seem to notice; he kissed the animal next to its closed eyelid and felt the heavy breathing. In. Then out. Calm. The boy went back to his saddlebag and brought out a blanket that his mother had made for him long ago. It was dirty and blackened and he brought it over to where he had been sitting. He lifted the blanket, warm and dry still, to his face and breathed in the familiar smell of home. He closed his eyes and could see his mother sitting by the furnace, rocking back and forth in her chair, cloth in her hands. He could remember her, as if she were there before her. In the distance, he could still hear the quiet cries of the world around him, calling for its salvation. And he closed his eyes and slept.

A hushed whimper made him open his eyes and lose track of his thoughts. It seemed to come from a ways down the river. The rain had slowed some but still fell heavily. He set down the blanket and picked up the rifle and walked quietly in the hazy and dark afternoon toward the sound, hiding himself behind a large flowering bush, the blooms of which seemed to show no color in the muted world he walked. He heard the sound again, this time louder and more distinct. It was the stifled cry of a woman. He walked down some twenty paces more, moving with the current towards the hushed cries that were becoming more frequent, though not louder. There, before him, prone on her back, lay a young woman, no older than he. Her body rolled back and forth as if swaying with the ebb and flow of the water that nearly lapped up onto her bare legs. A small marshland surrounded her with yellow and green grass and reeds jutting up from the stagnant and putrid water.

Her hair had been a reddish gold, but was now stained in dark and mud. She wore what once was a dress, its color all but consumed in time and the earth's pillaging, blackened and shredded in parts. From the position she lay, the dress had become pulled up near to her waist, the frayed and torn garment billowed about her body holding her immobile and secure, surrounding her body. Her legs and arms were a deep sunburned orange that seemed to stand out in the darkness and heaviness of the air; her thighs, however, were a pale milky white with blotches of deep oozing mud clumped. The rain continued down upon her, erupting the flowing water in tiny explosions and crashing with pelted thuds upon the wet and soggy ground surrounding her.

Josiah looked about him, back in the direction he had come and then downriver, and then back at the young woman. He took a few more steps forward, lowering the rifle and setting it propped against a thicket of felled branches from the overhanging trees. He stepped out into the rain and felt it soak his body, his clothes clinging to his skin, weighing him down. The young woman had her eyes closed as she moved about, as if in a trance: thrashing and then settling her arms back at her sides before resuming their restless movement. It wasn't until he was a few feet from her that he noticed the cream colored bundle tucked in the curve of her body, beneath her arms, as if clinging onto her. He slowed his steps and saw that the bundle was that of a newborn. It lay still, nestled in the young woman's flowing dress skirt. Its head was bloated and bluish and clean, save for the spackling of grime from the rain and dirt that lacquered it in an earthy baptism. The tiny thing's body below the neck was fat and slick with afterbirth and blood, a mucous slickness to it. The boy stood for a time, not moving, not comprehending, only looking on to the newborn and its mother.

The young woman sat up hurriedly, as if sensing the boy's presence, and she turned to face him. Her face was swollen and red with emotion and although she continued to cry, there were no tears left and she only let out gasping wails into the dreary afternoon. She cradled the lifeless newborn in her lap, swaying with her body through her stammered cries. The boy took another step forward and then stopped. Her breath had become more strained the more she wept. Her body seemed to convulse. Spittle clung to her lower lip. Through the sobs, she spoke to the boy, staring into his face in search of some light in her darkness. "I wanted it to happen. I wanted it." Her lips curved into a slight smile and then she looked off down the river and wiped her face with the back of her hand, leaving dirt marks on her cheek. She whispered to herself: "I wanted it."

Josiah walked over to the young woman and knelt beside her and looked down at the form lying on her lap. A wet coating of liquid and mucous was on the skin, the cord, like rough sinew, was still stretching from its middle. The newborn's body rose and fell with the rapid breath of its mother, seeming to twitch and move, although it was only a mirage to the boy. Rain water splashed all about them, crashing onto their skin and running down in long painted streaks to the ground. The steady thump of water on skin sounded, and bugs danced in their flight, landing momentarily on the skin of the newborn, only to tread the sticky flesh and fly off again. The boy looked uneasily at the newborn, watching the water land and each drop begin to wash away the bloody and slick varnish of the flesh.

The young woman looked back at Josiah; panic seemed to flood over her. She had stopped weeping and instead of sadness fear had now entered onto her face. "Don't curse me. Please. Don't curse me. Don't hurt me." She pleaded to him. "It ain't my fault. He come to me. He did. I couldn't . . . Evil, that's what it was. Evil. It was his. He did it to me. He did. I never wanted none of it. It ain't my fault. Believe me."

The boy sat on the ground next to her and placed his hand on her shivering arm. It was cold and moist, and the rain continued to fall. Her dress was covered in blood, turned an organic tinge of red and brown that seemed to be borne from the dirt of the earth. "Who?" he asked quietly.

She looked to the newborn in her lap and then to Josiah and took a strange, deep breath that seemed foreign even to her. "The devil," she said. Her voice seemed to have gathered an unknown strength. "He come to me one night, he come to me an he put this thing inside me, this devil baby. Thought it was a dream. But it felt real. He come an he hold down my hands an arms an he was lookin at me with his face an I felt his breath on me an, my sweet Jesus, it was the most horrid thing I ever saw. Disgustin. His face was like a mask, but not." She paused and began to stroke the clammy skin of the newborn in her lap.

Josiah looked down at the newborn in the young woman's lap. He thought he saw the eyes of the newborn move under their closed lids, and he watched them for a while longer but they did not move, and he looked back at the woman.

She continued: "I was scared, but still thought it all a dream, but then I grew fatter an fatter an they tell me I can't never live in their house no more havin child out of wed an me bein so young. An they called me a whore, a harlot from the Bible times, tellin me I ain't their child no more. But I ain't never been with no one before, cept that night. But it was a dream." She paused, closing her eyes and wiping tears away with her grimed hands. "His face—I still see it when I close my eyes—burns my eyelids still. An I knowed it was him. I knowed it." Her voice drifted away, caught in the wind, taken somewhere entirely different from here and from now. "It wasn't even the face, but the eyes. I could tell from the eyes. They was little eyes, no white in em. No, they was dark, like holes in his head but he was lookin out at me, seein me the whole while. And his face . . ." She shook her head, letting her hair loosen in the wind then settle back to her shoulders, heavy and tired. "There wasn't no face to him. Face looked burned off like in hell's fire. No nose, no hair. Jus skin. Little mouth barely moved, but he didn't say nothin. Little bits of hair on his head, black strings. It was him. I knowed it. He ain't had but no face an his skin was all wet an sticky an hot, seemed to burn me with his touch."

The boy turned away and watched the water of the river pass by where they sat. He took a deep breath and then exhaled. He looked back at her, his hand resting gently now on her shoulder. She continued, as if she were talking to herself: "An I could not move. I could not move. He held my arms down while he done it.

An I screamed so loud, I tried to, but ain't no sound but a whisper come out an he kept to it an I could hear his breathin an feel it an smell the awful smell of his breath an I cried an cried but I couldn't move. An finally I remember jus seein black an everthin else seemed to stop an then I woke up, still sweatin and still cryin.

"An I got bigger an bigger. An when time come today fer it, I didn't know what I was gonna do, but by God's mercy I found myself here next to this here water, an when it come out I took it an without twice thought, I took its head an stuck it under til the feet stopped movin. An it kicked an was movin its arms all bout an I could hear it screamin under the rushin water here, an I cried but I kept it there until it went still." Her lips began to tremble as she took the newborn's tiny hand, still covered in its congealed coating, in hers. The small hand disappeared in hers, and Josiah felt a sense of security and peace with those two hands. She looked at Josiah. "An when it stopped movin I sat here wonder what I was an what I done. An I don't know the answer. I don't know." She turned and placed her raw hand on Josiah's and gripped it tight, squeezing it, "What am I?"

Josiah shook his head slowly. "I don't know."

She looked at the flowing water of the river. "I need God's forgiveness."

Josiah nodded his head silently and then looked once more at the small newborn lying still on the ground between her opened legs where it had just fallen.

"Forgive me," she said. "Please. Forgive me."

And Josiah sat there silently, his hand caressing the young woman's shoulders as he watched her draw the newborn close to her sweat and pain drenched bosom, sharing her warmth with it, in some way hoping that it would awaken from its slumber and call out to her.

Beyond them, the river flowed peacefully while the rain continued to fall.

The rain and thunder were chasing themselves from the evening sky when The Rider entered the small, ruined town, an effigy to a prior prosperous civilization's inhabitation, now only a derelict façade of what it had been. Scattered puddles were collected and shined in the moon's glow, starting the slow process of self destruction in the autumn evening. The few wooden buildings looked either decaying or dead in the night's haze and all things around The Rider looked haggard and rotting. A monotoned groan seemed to escape the structures, as if they were crying out in horror from the pain that they sheltered.

He walked the black horse slowly through the main street, his eyes casually looking over the barren side streets and roads. Stark and abandoned. High clouds passed overhead, throwing the town into shadows and scattered light. The main street stretched and rounded off to the right, passing a hotel and saloon and continuing on to more shops and the market area. Many of the buildings were constructed of a dirty brick that once had been red but now was more black than anything else. The Rider's eyes felt heavy and his body exhausted. As he dismounted from the horse and tethered the leather strap to the post outside the hotel, he noticed the faint glow of light from beyond the street's curve and he heard the hushed drone of whispers.

The Rider walked toward the light, coming to the curve of the street and then following it around its bend. He saw the source of the light: torches held high in the darkness, attached to tall poles and stakes that stretched deep into the ground, and there below, in the light's glow, stood the townspeople. Some were holding more flaming torches, some holding guns, others holding children close to their own bodies. They all looked like a horde of simpletons and miscreants gathered in the night, ready to make battle with some mythic enemy. The Rider walked slowly down the dusty street in the direction of the crowd. Large pebbles and rocks were strewn here and there, discarded. He walked with his right hand resting on the warm butt of the revolver at his side, his coat pulled slightly back, tucked and hidden by his arm.

The townspeople were gathered in front of a large, crude stage:

wooden planks staggered some ten feet in length on top of a base some four or five feet tall. The Rider stopped a few feet from the outer darkened edge of the mass and listened intently to the quiet that now spread throughout them all.

To the right of the stage, hidden in shadows, was a tent from which a heavy man emerged and climbed the stairs to the platform and stood before the gathering that remained hushed in the reverential silence. The Rider looked at the faces of these men and women and saw in them all the look of anticipation for something unknown or secret. The heavy man stood, unmoving for a time unknown; he simply remained still, looking out into the darkness of the void that only exists between performer and audience. A disquieting expectancy seemed to surge through the crowd; people turned their gazes upon each other in confusion, then back to the lone performer on the stage before them. For some, this dance of their eyes seemed to continue on without cease.

The heavy man was dressed in loose fitting purple sheets that dangled from his limp arms and gathered in a bundle at his feet. His head was shaved bald, the torchlight reflecting off of it dimly. A murmured hush began to rise from the waiting crowd, sounding like a swarm of winged insects rising from some marshy bog until the lone man on stage raised his arms high above him, throwing the audience into an abrupt silence.

The performer stood motionless, his arms stretched high to the darkened heavens. After several seconds, four more performers climbed the steps to join him. Each of these performers carried tall torches that threw the stage into shadows; each performer wore brilliant wooden masks adorned with shimmering jewelry, which gleamed in the light, and long flowing red tunics and capes. The performers circled about the bald man, his figure dancing and turning on the stage, his shadows cast out upon the audience and on the fronts of the stores and structures of the town street.

The flames whipped this way and that until each of the four performers stopped and stretched each flame as high as they could reach. The heavy man knelt down on the stage and rubbed his hands over his shimmering head, then lay facedown on the stage. A steady and low sounding chant escaped from the other performers, growing louder and more forceful as they went; the body of the first man began to writhe on the ground, first as if in agony, then as if in a euphoric climax. Then the chanting stopped, only to continue in the minds of the gathered audience, and the heavy man stopped his thrashing and remained, once again, motionless and quiet.

From the darkness of the corners of the stage, two more performers appeared and walked toward the heavy man and grabbed him by his arms and brought him to his feet. His eyes seemed to be filled with tears, dark makeup streaked down his cheeks, his face and bald skull red, coated now in sweat. His arms dangled at their sides as the two performers pushed and pulled the lifeless body of the first in a macabre dance. Along the border of the stage, the other performers began to sway slowly with their torches, shadow-demons being created on the lighted stage and then disappearing only to reappear in some other unguarded corner of the night.

The heavy man lifted his eyes up to the stars and moved his mouth, uttering an unheard prayer of thanks or forgiveness or both. The two performers on either side of him backed away and pulled from beneath their tunic wardrobe black whips that they began to circle over their heads and then crack down over the heavy man's back. The bald man jarred with each crack as if the leather was actually connecting with his back, his skin being split, yet he did not cry out, but stood erect. After a dozen cracks of the whips, the heavy man raised his arms to his sides and then forward, his palms extended outward to the crowd. Behind him, the chorus of torches converged into one, lighting a large structure in the back of the stage that sparked and ignited and burned bright in the dark. The flames spread quickly, revealing a cross that seared itself in the minds of the audience members whose mouths were agape at the brilliant devastation. Those performers who had been carrying torches seemed to disappear from the stage and only the single man remained.

As the flames from the cross behind him grew brighter, he lowered his arms and swiftly, with a practiced gesture, shrugged off the sheets, letting them fall to his feet, exposing an obese body covered in only a white cloth over his crotch and red paint covering, in streaked formation, his entire body. He spread his arms back out to where they had been, his head once again searching the stars above him before it lolled down to his chest, heavy and lifeless.

From the edge of the crowd, The Rider watched the play, a subtle smile on his face. He turned to leave but he was brought back by the deep rumblings of a voice from the stage. There, instead of the performers stood a gangly man, his hair white in the firelight, a big moustache stretching out past his cheeks. "As town judge I here declare that tomorrow morning, come nine o'clock, we will have the hanging of the three men convicted of the robbery of the town bank and grocer and the killing of our dear friend Lazarus Tompkins." The judge looked down at a piece of paper in his hand and announced the names of the three condemned men with a tone of authority and pride. "I invite you to come on out and see justice be done."

The Rider turned and left the crowd behind him and walked back to the hotel, his head bowed in thought.

He felt her breath hot and wet on the skin of his neck and he began to kiss her brown skin and drag his tongue over the small variations and contours of her body. And then he found her open and waiting mouth and he kissed her, tasting her hot saliva and feeling the softness of her tongue. He felt his penis grow more erect and he ran his fingers through her hair and over her small ears, and this sent quiet waves of shivers down her body and caused bumps to form on her arms and neck and he covered her skin with his and warmed her, making the bumps vanish. Her breathing became shallower and more strained and when he brushed his fingers gently over her brown nipples she began to moan gently into his ear and tell him how she wanted him to be inside of her.

After he came, they lay together, their bodies still one. And they remained that way for a while, laying in the cool moonlight that came in from the open window, and the candle's light that cast their ethereal shadows on the walls and the ceiling—their giant doubles that seemed to move this way and that of their own free will, their shadowed bodies still entwined in the passions of love.

She stared into his eyes, as if she were looking past his skin and through his body and into some hidden area that even he was kept from, and she continued to look at him without turning away, without wavering, without word. And he gently brushed the black hair back from her face, letting her eyes become heavier and heavier still until she closed them completely and fell asleep. He continued to look at her into the early parts of the night, feeling how still she was a mystery to him, something he so desperately wanted to understand and know completely. This dark woman. This woman from the earth.

The ghosts of past events seemed to sweep through the dirty streets of the town and surround the audience waiting in the early morning cold; these forgotten things cascading down and blowing through each man and woman, each child and elder like a solitary lament moving along on the wisps of the morning when all shadow passes to light and dark is overcome again. These memories that forever linger in the heavens, removed from some other distant time that cannot be recalled, except by the air and the breeze and the wind, and only briefly then.

The townspeople all stood, gathered together as they had the previous night, all rising with the sun and joining one another in front of the hangman and his trade materials. The gallows stood erect, lingering in the morning light. Heavy shadows were cast upon those people nearest the stage floor. The high wooden beam stood alone on the stage, empty and forgetful of the lives it had already taken.

There was twice the number of townspeople as had showed for the play the night before; it seemed as if they had manifested and multiplied themselves from the dust of the earth in creation. The crowd stretched back, far into the street, past where the players' stage had been erected some hours before. The street showed no sign of the stage or the players that had inhabited it, and if you hadn't known better, you would not have known it had ever existed.

The empty ropes hung low from a beam some eight feet above the stage floor. Beneath each swinging noose was a wooden box two feet or so in length and height. In the morning breeze, the ropes swayed back and forth, drifting like steady pendulums that were simply counting the seconds of the day's remainder. Far from the stage, past where the crowd stretched, The Rider sat tall on his horse; the animal stamped fitfully at the dusty ground. He watched as the crowd congealed and moved together in one mass, many parts forming one—one breath, one heartbeat, one soul, even. The Rider's eyes narrowed under the dark shadowing brim of his hat.

He turned behind him and watched as a slow procession made its way toward the crowd: three men shuffled their bare and dirty feet, stirring the dust into the air in a dull scraping ring— static in the silence of the street around them. Each man's hair was long and matted to their heads; their hands were tied by chains behind their backs and the loose rags of clothing barely held on to each of their gaunt and bony frames. The three of them looked to be brothers, all cast from some same mold with only slight variations in their complexions and actions to show any distinction between one and the next.

The grotesque three were led by a large man in a dark hat, and they were all followed by a thin and wiry man with a rifle pointed ceremoniously at the heels of the chained man in front of him. Both the man in the front and the one in the back of the group held their heads high and proud, subtle smirks spread across their cheeks.

Looking at either one, you would expect him to begin laughing at any moment. As if by sense, the crowd began to part, separating into two seething forms, waiting in aggravated expectancy of the filth and evil that would pass within and between their parted sea. Insults and jeers were screamed from the crowd. A stench of sweat and piss fouled the air. All eyes were set upon the coming procession, and The Rider turned on his saddle to watch them.

The five men made their way through the assembly of onlookers, the middle three of the procession dodging every so often backward from something thrown from the crowd, usually sharp rocks and eggs. They soon came to the steps at the front of the stage and mounted them slowly, their eyes kept down in either shame or anger. They were helped up to the platform of the stage by their two previous escorts. When they reached the top of the steps, the three men stood before the crazed onlookers. Their eyes remained down, as if they were studying their own dirty feet and the color of the wood that they stood on. They spread out from each other so that they were a few steps apart. The two preceding escorts made their way to opposite sides of the stage, standing on either end of the row of condemned men. Each man on the small stage looked out quietly at the gathered townspeople.

The jeers and insults continued from the townspeople as two other men climbed the stairs of the stage and stood before the three condemned; these men's backs were to the crowd and both of them wore black. The younger of these two men wore a long frock that reached down to the ground and a dark wide hat that seemed to curl down on each side from the heavy weight of the fabric, casting his clean shaven face in complete shadow. In his right hand, this man held a large black leather Bible, and in his left hand he held a large cross that could have been mistaken for a weapon, from medieval times or from the future. The second man wore a long black shirt and a smaller black hat that turned up on either side of his head, exposing large, red ears. This man was older than the first and he had a dark beard that stretched down past the neck line of his shirt. His feet were covered by high, black leather boots and the spurs that were attached to the back of them showed brightly in the sun, blinding a portion of the crowd with every step he took.

The crowd quieted only briefly as the younger man talked with each of the condemned quietly and moved the cross in front of each man's face separately—up, down, side, side—and he allowed each man to kiss or spit on the relic. Once he finished, the young man dismounted the steps and walked off, moving into the rising shouts from the crowd protesting the giving of last rights to scum and dirt. When The Rider looked for the priest, he found that the man had disappeared.

The older one of the two, the bearded man, leaned in and whispered something to the three straggled men that stood still, facing out to the crowd. After the man leaned away from them, they each stepped up onto the splintered wooden boxes behind them, their hands still tied behind their backs by the chains. They balanced themselves on the narrow boxes; one of them had to step back down and then step up again to keep from falling off. The wood felt hot on their dirty, bare feet. The angry insults and comments from the crowd began to escalate into shouts and screams. Some of the women were in tears, tugging at their long black dresses. Children were holding their ears to block the rising noise, their faces contorted in confusion and fear. A steadying tension was mounting into something that seemed confusing to The Rider—it was as if the anger at these men was fabricated, made of something guttural and raw that each person had been keeping deep within their own souls, an anger that they each were now simply taking out on these three. The Rider looked around at the faces, red with heat and rage, and he thought he could only see a semblance of real hatred at the condemned three.

And they stood on their boxes without moving, waiting for the judgment that was about to be brought upon them. The man in the center wept, his head hanging down. His sobs became lost in the screaming that surrounded the place. The two men on either side were looking up to the sky; the man on the right moved his mouth in silent and secret prayer, a prayer without sound or words that no one could hear except for himself and the wind. The man on the left had turned up his face as if he were going to sneeze, but he did not. He shook his head slowly and it seemed as if he were laughing at the situation and then he looked out at the jeering townspeople.

The bearded man turned from the three men. He spread his arms out wide, hushing the crowd. He called out, his voice bellowing and quieting the crowd: "Bag em or watch their faces? Up to you."

A chorus of "Watch em" rang out in the morning.

The bearded man nodded and turned, saying something more to the three men, and then he moved behind them, draping the dangling rope nooses around each of the three's necks. He barely needed to stand on his toes to reach the ropes. And he tightened each knot, his manners grandiose, as if he were a magician or showman selling a product. Once the ropes were fitted, the bearded man walked behind the man on the left and, without ceremony or warning, kicked the wooden box out, letting it fly out to the edge of the stage. The condemned man's body dropped quickly and jerked, his hair swirling about his suspended body. Many of the viewers sighed in regret that the neck snapped before he could strangle himself to death.

Without any pause, the bearded man moved over, past the middle man, to the man on the right and kicked the box out. The box flew from the stage and landed loudly just before the gathered men and women. The crowd gasped, some laughing aloud as the dangling man kicked his frail legs, jerking the whole of the rope and his body with it. The beam overhead grunted from the strain but it held strong. The man's eyes bulged and stood out from his skull, his face a bright red, his cheeks puffed out. Short choppy grunts escaped from his throat. He twisted slowly in the air, his breath escaping him. He kicked hard with his feet, trying to find something below him to stand on but there was nothing and after several minutes he simply dangled there, and did not move anymore except for the turning of the rope.

The bearded man walked over and rested his foot on the box on which the middle convict stood. The bearded man raised his hand to his ear mockingly, taunting the crowd, and the crowd responded with screams of excitement.

The Rider moved the horse closer to the stage. He could hear the people silently cursing the three men still. He looked back to the stage. The bearded man now stood a distance behind the middle man, and he now had a long, thin strap of leather in his hand that seemed to have manifested itself there magically. The loud snap of the leather on the condemned man's back sounded loudly, drowning out the screams of the townspeople. The man screamed out and then again as the bearded man brought the leather strap down on the man's back again and again. The man's shirt began to rip and red welts formed, on his skin. It wasn't until the bearded man broke skin with the strap and blood began to flow from the marks that the bearded man stopped and let go of the leather piece. He was out of breath and knelt down to collect himself. Sweat formed on his forehead and ran down his face, and then he stood tall and nodded to the crowd, who seemed to scream louder now. The condemned man's body looked limp, barely standing erect on the box, tears painting themselves on his cheeks. His body shuddered every so often in a spasm of motion that was the only thing that notified to the crowd that he was still alive.

The bearded man walked slowly around the dangling body of the left man and stood before the one in the middle. He balled his fist up tightly and plunged it into the gut of the middle man who lost his balance and fell off the box, swinging back and forth, his feet moving frantically trying to stand back on the box. The bearded man stood in front of the hanging man and slowly scraped the box further out of reach of his feet and then walked off the stage, leaving the crowd to enjoy this man's last moments pass. The hanging man's eyes nearly escaped their sockets—they were blood red and veined. The neck skin around the rope was bleeding from where the rope cut into it, and it was turning a deep purple and yellow. After several minutes, the three men hung in unison, ornamental chimes in the wind that moved slowly and peacefully in the breeze. Their faces were blue and lifeless. To The Rider, they looked to be demonic puppets on a hellish stage, mere sideshow amusements to a clamorous and applauding audience.

Without looking back at the crowd, The Rider turned his horse in the opposite direction of the stage and kicked it twice, leaving a faint trail of dust that no one noticed.

In some far reached corner of the land children play games of hide and seek and a mother's child is born. Seconds pass and move and stream by in some wakeful melody as it has for time unmeasured. A single leaf bud springs anew from the dark cracks of the skin and stretches its blossom ever higher to the sun and voices sing in chant and harmony and reconfiguration to the tunes of the sea that seem to be consuming heaven's own dreams. And this all happens in not just some far off place imagined, but it is scattered abundantly over every direction and path and land and people, and there is hope and there is peace and there is love, if but only for a few moments in time and time again.

Josiah Fuller

I can remember the day my father taught me to hold an shoot a gun when I was little. He took me out there out back of our house an he held that gun up with me, his arms around me like a hug, an he showed me where to put my head, an he told me to close my eyes, an take a breath an then let it out fore pullin the trigger of it. I can remember the first time I shot the gun myself—it was at a big tree that had fallen the year before. An I remember that gun an how it shot back hard at me, hurtin my face an my shoulder. I almost dropped the thing. But I can still see him clappin an laughin, an I remember going back inside an tellin my mother . . . I miss em. Never thought I could feel such an emptiness inside me. I keep imaginin that I know what I'm doin here, but I don't really. I wish I did. I wish I could believe in God an heaven an hell. I used to, but I can't no more. Not after seein em swingin like that. Not after I cut em down an buried they black bodies, smellin so bad I couldn't move none, couldn't see nothin through my cryin. It only stopped after I covered em up with dirt . . . I tell myself stories a lot of the time now, when I ain't got no one round me to talk to. I reckon that's what stories are. I reckon it's how people survive in this world—they make up stories and beliefs, traditions an ways of doin things that are both true and not true, an all of it is so that people can forget what it is that life really is about. They lie to themselves to help them get through it all. That's what I reckon anyhow . . . I hope to find him, I do. But I also don't want to. I'm not sure I'd know what to do when I actually saw him. Suppose I can only remember what my father taught me: lift it high, aim it, breathe out, an then pull the trigger. Only thing left to do, I reckon.

5

A splinter in the wood has begun its preordained laceration of the bark. The charred out-regions of the massive block stand, still smoking from heaven's flame, and the innards are black and coal red and feel hot to the touch. When the rain touches it, a hissing sting erupts softly only to be drowned by the rain's handprints on the earth around the remains. The blackened and dead form stands alone, weakened to its knees, and all around the gray skyline erupts still with blasts of energy and fire, and the echoing sound drifts from far away and the rain mixes with the black and white ash of the surrounds and creates a milky paste of war paint.

The morning was just about to break as The Rider lifted his face from the earth. He had been praying, but he whispered Amen and then stood and looked at the sky, watching the faint streaks of color show. He walked over to the horse and climbed on, his movements stagnant and pained. He wrapped a blanket around his shivering body and they, horse and rider, began to head south.

He had not ridden far when he came to a thick clustering of trees. He climbed off the horse and drew the blanket tighter around his still cold body. The sun was just beginning its ascent and the world was still dark.

He walked to the edge of the trees and then he felt it: the steady rumbling movement that seemed to originate within the earth's core and spread outward from there. His legs felt the shake and he knelt down and put his hand on the cold and wet ground and his hand, too, registered the steady quaking of the dark land. He stood and began to walk through the thicket of cedars and pines, whose colored leaves could not be deciphered in the coming light of the morning, and stopped at the edge of a giant expanse of land. Before him stretched a large clearing, completely removed of tree or bush or life.

Running through this area were two lines of steel rail that stretched endlessly off into the east. He followed the rails along for several yards, heading west, feeling the more violent jolts of the approaching train as he walked on. Eventually, he came to a gradual bend in the rails that led to the north. And here, at this bend, he saw another set of rails that diverged from the ones he had been following along, these new rails continued on to the west. The two different rails connected in an inverted "Y" from where The Rider was standing. These new western-directed rails looked newer, brighter somehow. He followed these new rails along and saw that they led toward a large mountain and he imagined that if he were to continue along them that they would direct him around the mountain and on into the mysteries of the west, through the plains and grass fields, over and around mountains and past animals, known and imagined, and finally on to the Pacific.

Behind him sounded the heavy whistle of the train, and when it sounded dozens of birds escaped from the seclusion of the surrounding trees where they had been hiding and they flew off together creating a black spot in the sky that moved in various directions but seemed to carry on as if it were one. The Rider moved into the trees and after several minutes he watched as the train passed by him, moving along the tracks quickly and continuing on to the north.

From the passing train, The Rider would have looked simply as another tree that stood guarding the rail tracks. Several dozen cars were attached to the front engine, and in the exposed beds of each car was heaped stacks of coal and lumber that passed by in dark lines that blurred together in the early morning.

William Corvin walked out into the sepia dawn of the morning.

The first faint breaths of light were rising forth over the slopes in the distance, over the rolling hills tucked between the high walls of the valley. He walked over to the barn and stable area, across the grass clearing, toward the shuffling sound of horse hoofs on the dry and brittle ground. Above him a hawk passed and he looked up but could only see the bird in the distance, a small rodent held in its clutches.

He dragged open the doors that had been made heavy with the rain. The wood of the doors smelled sour and he turned his face away. Shadows were beginning to stretch forth in the room, light invading through the loosened slats along the sides and roof of the barn. He could see dust particles and such dancing in the beams, a phosphorescent shimmer igniting itself within the stale air.

The horses shuddered loudly in their pens and he could hear their heavy breaths. He called out a good morning. In the far corner of the barn a lantern was lighted and a door opened and shut and toward him walked a black man who was in his forties but looked to be nearer to sixty years old. The negro was dressed in a long, white shirt and jean pants made filthy by time and dirt. On his feet he wore a pair of new, tan boots. He was scratching his graying head and shaking his arms to break them from the rigidness of sleep. The negro called forth a good morning back to Corvin and bent down and picked up a lighted lantern that threw strange shapes on the walls and floor of the barn.

Corvin walked over to one of the horses and patted the animal's head and rubbed his hand over the animal's long and coarse body. He could feel the rounded rib bones under the hair and skin. He took off the blanket that had been draped over the horse's back and was beginning to place the saddle on the animal when the negro man came and hung the lantern on a nail peg hammered into the wooden side of the pen. This man helped with the leather straps, buckling them tight and fitting the metal bit in the horse's mouth and tying the loosened ends up and out of the way. "Mornin, Jefferson," Corvin said.

"Where you off to this mornin, sir?" Jefferson folded up the blanket and set it on the straw and hay covered ground and walked with the man outside, the latter leading the horse.

"Check up on the mines, I suppose. New load supposed to go out this mornin. Probably gone by now already."

"Missus ain't comin wit yeh?"

"Not feelin too well."

Jefferson nodded and looked off to the distance.

Corvin sat up on the horse and led it around the clearing before returning back to Jefferson. He looked down at the negro. "Keep an eye on her. All right? Check up. Don't allow her to do nothin too foolish."

Jefferson smiled up at the man. "Don't reckon she'd listen much to me, but I can try."

Corvin smiled down at Jefferson and then rode off.

Jefferson watched him disappear into the breaking morning and then he turned back to the barn and stable to feed the other horses and begin the day's work.

The two men came upon the camp in the early parts of the morning when there were still shadows left over from the night previous. They had heard a series of explosions hours before while they slept and they had woken and begun walking the distance of several miles to the camp, guided only by the steady sound of scraping and pounding metal and the random explosion that would silence all sounds before and after it for several minutes.

The journey had taken them through different parts of the woods that they had not been through before and they had watched the sun rise and fix itself above them. They eventually reached the outer rim of the camp, and from where they were, they looked in and watched the bustling of men and women here and there as if they were programmed by some higher being, sentenced to do his bidding. Some of the people in the camp pushed wheelbarrows filled with metal spikes or other tools and equipment while others carried axes or shovels.

The two men hid behind two trees and after several minutes

of watching, the taller of the two began to walk out from behind the cover of the tree and into the camp. This man turned and looked back at the other man, who was still hiding in the shadows. "Wilkins," the first man called back. "Let's go."

Wilkins shook his head. "I ain't goin out there, Cooper. They'll see us."

Cooper turned and walked back to Wilkins. "You hungry, ain't yeh?" he asked.

Wilkins nodded quietly. His eyes were set to the ground; every few seconds he would look up, past Cooper, to the people that were walking freely in the camp.

"Well, so am I. Now, let's go get in there and grab us some food and get out. Ain't nobody gonna give a shit bout us if we look like we oughta be here. Now let's get."

They made their way through the camp. A thin layer of dust seemed to be settled permanently about the place and the different people they passed—mostly men but some women and smaller children could be found, as well; they were all coated a light brown color. The people looked to be a foreign race of people from origins unknown, their skin looking to be pasted over, a replica of the earth.

To the west of where Cooper and Wilkins were, in the direction they now walked, was a high, flat rock that stretched several hundred feet into the clear sky of the day. It was mostly gray and black rock, but some parts of it were lined with trees and bushes that grew from the side, seemingly contradicting both the science of man and of nature. Cooper looked up at the mountain. On its highest point, he could see a hanging cliff that stretched out over its base several dozen feet. From below, it looked like a giant beak on the top of a monolithic stone beast. Cooper looked back down at the road they walked, little wider than a cart path.

As the two men continued to walk, they could hear the steady clanging sound of metal, and they turned their attention to the east and saw various rows of twenty or thirty men, most of them black, their skin also tarnished to a pastel lightness by the dust.

Each of these men was holding onto a piece of chain that was fitted around a long metal rail. Some of the rows were helped by horses or mules that had the chains attached to them. In each row, the men pulled in unison, dragging the metal railing through the dust, and setting it in front of another rail of equal size and length. After this, they let the chain drop and they each set to work hammering long spikes into the ground to connect the different rail pieces together. Some of the men would, at times, go over to one of the numerous wheelbarrows or carts to get more spikes or a drink of water and then return to where they had come, their tools held tightly in their worn and calloused hands.

"Railroad comin through here now," Wilkins whispered under his breath.

Off to the west, leading up toward the rock mountain, was a long line of light colored tents that had been stained by the dust and the winds and the rain. These tents were made of a heavy canvas that held its shape when the wind came through.

Cooper and Wilkins walked over and entered one of the tents and found two padded cots, each with a small blanket folded neatly and set on its top. They entered another tent and found a similar layout, although on one of the cots here the blanket was still spread out over the bed and spilled down onto the dusty ground. Next to this cot was a small, brown bag. Wilkins smiled and let out a low chuckle and then grabbed the blanket and the bag, stuffed the blanket inside, and hid both under his coat. They looked around the small tent quickly for anything else they might need, but seeing nothing of use, they walked out of the tent, bending low.

After searching several other tents and finding only small things to take—a pocket watch that didn't tick, some coins, a long sleeved shirt—the two men entered a larger tent. Wooden baskets and metal pails lined the edges of the tent and each held dozens of different fruits, dried and fresh, and loaves of bread. Wilkins filled the bag quickly, stuffing it full with several apples and some different kinds of berries and five or six loaves of bread.

He tied the bag shut and then slung it over his shoulder and the two men walked out of the tent and headed down the path toward the birdlike mountain to the west.

They had only walked a few steps before they heard the shouts and screams of dozens of men, the voices sounding foreign to the two men. They looked and saw, near to the base of the massive rock, men and women running franticly back and forth. A few seconds later a thunderous sound ignited in the air and swept through the whole place and out into the world. The ground rumbled below their feet and they saw a thick cloud of smoke rise into the air from the foot of the mountain. Cooper and Wilkins each clasped their hands to their ears and shied away, staying in such manner for several seconds after the sound disappeared. After the devastating echo finished they looked at each other and removed their hands from their ears and hurried forward to see what the explosion came from.

A fifty foot by forty foot tunnel had been carved into the bottom of the rock mountain. A running pair of metal rails, long and stretching, led directly into the tunnel, disappearing in the darkness of the thing.

Dozens of men were running deep within the tunnel, some were carrying out rock pieces from the inside—the rocks ranging from what looked to be mere pebbles to small boulders that were four or five feet in diameter and needed to be carried by two men. Other men were coming from the tunnel carrying stacks of a dark material inside. After a few minutes of this, the two men heard the cries for evacuation and, once again, saw the chaotic running of men and women and finally they saw and heard the next explosion. Rocks and other pieces of earth rolled down the mountain side, black rock was blasted from inside the tunnel out, and smoke seeped from the tunnel's entrance. Eventually the ground quit its shaking and the earth was quiet and steady again, even if only for a few moments.

The two men turned to the north to leave the camp area. Wilkins was smiling wide and Cooper looked at him and shook his head. There were more tents stretched off to the north, and on their way out of the place Wilkins stopped at one of these tents and went in and a few seconds later came back out without saying anything and joined Cooper and they walked through the rest of the camp in silence.

They did not realize it on their way out of the place, but inside one of the unmarked tents along the stretch they walked lay an old man on one of the cots. Both of this man's legs were missing after having been crushed by a falling boulder after one of the blasts. The camp surgeon had shaken his head when he made the final cuts on the destroyed limbs hours earlier. This man lay still, struggling with every breath, and he looked up to the top of the tent. No one heard as this man called out in supplication to his God in a tongue unknown to any of the other men or women in the camp. Hours later, this man would die. The surgeon would come to check on the patient and the man's mouth would be open, along with one of his eyes, his hands would be folded together in a peaceful position of prayer over his chest, and the cot that he lay on would be soaked through with the now cold blood that would come from the stitchings and through the wrappings on the man's thighs.

It was not until a half mile or so out of the small rail camp that the two men stopped again to rest and Cooper asked Wilkins what he had taken from the last tent. Wilkins smiled and reached into the brown bag that still hung from his shoulder and took out one of the black sticks that they had seen the men at the camp carrying into the heart of the mountain.

"In case," Wilkins said. He replaced it in the bag and then smiled again. The other man shook his head.

They walked deeper into the woods, leaving the outer regions of the camp far behind them. And as they walked, Cooper and Wilkins paid no notice to the hundreds of felled and cut trees that lay scattered about the wilderness for miles in each direction. These trees and what was left of them lay here and there like cast off flotsam and jetsam, amorphous bodies that had been struck down in battle and left to rot. And high on the rock mountain, a hawk was perched on a branch and looked down at the riven trees and the contabescent land. It looked down at the world like a gargoyle that could do nothing but witness the destruction of its home.

Only a few moments later another explosion sounded and the ground shook and the hawk set off in flight to some different place. Like so many now, the hawk was made a gypsy on some unspoken journey with no clear direction of where next to go.

The boy led the horse on foot into the small town. It was busy and people were moving quickly about as if some great commotion were happening or had just passed. A dozen or more women and children were gathered around a small market area where merchants were selling fruit and vegetables grown from their own personal gardens. There was a man and woman trying to sell dried meat, slabs of brown and pink sheets hanging from a line behind them. Other merchants were selling homemade trinkets that some of the shopping women were admiring in the sunlight.

After walking past the market area and hearing some of the women trying to barter prices, offering other goods that they had in their bags as trade for the fruits and vegetables, Josiah walked the horse to a trough off the main road. He dipped his hands in the cold water and then brought a handful up to his mouth and drank and then did so several times again. The water hurt his throat, but he continued to slurp at the water and then he brought several handfuls up to his face to wash the dirt and grime from it and then he scrubbed his hands together over the dirt and washed them again in the water. He looked around the town as the horse drank beside him.

As he led the horse back out onto the main road he saw, not far up ahead, a large platform being dismantled by six or seven men. He asked a woman who has holding the hand of a small child what was happening with the stage and she told him that there was a hanging of three men the previous day and that they were taking the stage down. He asked what had happened with the three men and she answered that they were off being buried in the ground out in the woods a distance away from the town. The boy nodded and then looked back at the stage. The child with the woman looked up at Josiah and smiled, and he looked down to see the child and he smiled back and thanked the two. Down from where the market was he saw the cracked sign of a hotel and restaurant and he led the horse to the hotel. He tied the horse to the post that was just in front of the entryway of the hotel and then took his gun from its sleeve on the saddle. He walked inside and looked around the place. To his left was the small eating area and he went over to it.

The small room was full of men. It wasn't until he looked at the darker corners of the room that Josiah saw the women: whores, most of them, each wearing white lace and red satin that seemed to shimmer even in the faint light of the place. When he saw them, he felt a tightening in his stomach that seemed to move itself out through his chest and gut.

After several seconds of looking at the women, Josiah turned back to the tables in the middle of the room. At almost every one were two or three men; some were eating breakfast, while others were drinking beer and whisky, talking quietly with one another. The room was dark, with only a thin stretch of sunlight coming in from the front windows. From this light, the people inside were cast in deep shadows and the light coming in seemed to lay a foundation over the darkened and muddy floors that had small holes burned through from dropped cigarettes and cigars. The boy walked up to the small bar area at the back of the room, making sure to keep his eyes from straying to the smiling women that lined the walls about him.

The barman asked what Josiah would have and the boy asked what the charge was for water. The barman smiled and poured Josiah a glass and set it before him. The boy thanked the man and then asked if there were any scraps of meat that he might have but the barman told him there was not and then walked away to fill the glass of a drunk man sitting on a stool down from the boy.

Josiah drank the water slowly. His stomach ached and he touched it with his hand only to feel bone and hardness. He could feel the cold dripping down from his throat and settling in his stomach, heavy.

"Ain't et fer awhile, has yeh?"

The boy turned and looked down the way, toward the corner of the room, and saw a man sitting at a small table by himself, his face cast in long, dark shadows—the only light around this man came from a cigarette that hung loosely in his mouth.

"Ain't et fer awhile?" the man repeated.

"You askin me?" the boy said, his voice barely sounding above a whisper.

"Well I ain't tellin yeh. You hungry I got some food I don't reckon I hardly can finish. It's yers if yeh want it."

The boy nodded.

The man shook his head and laughed quietly under his breath. "Yer gonna have to speak up fer me."

Josiah quietly said yes.

"Well, come on over and keep an old man company awhile." The man waved him over; his hands were covered in black leather gloves that seemed to become lost in the darkness of the wood behind him.

The boy picked up the gun and walked over to the man and sat. On the table was a plate full of eggs, some dried strips of black bacon, and bread. "All yers," the man said.

Josiah looked down at the food, his stomach making sounds, and then he sat and began to eat. His stomach hurt as he swallowed but he continued eating the food. Twice he began to choke and coughed up some of the food onto the plate and then put it back in his mouth. When he finished, he sat back in the chair and thanked the man.

"How long is it since yeh et, boy?" the man asked.

"Been some time."

"I can tell. Ain't heard a man et like that in many a years."

The man lit another cigarette. The flame of the match lighted the man's face briefly. Josiah couldn't make out the face but for a quick flash of light that seemed to spark from the man's eyes within the dark.

"I thank yeh." He looked around and then back to the man.

"How old are yeh? Sound no more than a youngin."

"Sixteen, seventeen. Don't know. Old nuff, I reckon."

"Are yeh? Old nuff fer what is the question, though." The man grinned. He tilted his head to one side and then back center; he seemed to look around the room, gazing up to the dark corners of the ceiling above as if he could hear phantoms conversing in the darkness.

"I reckon fer whatever it is I need to be ready fer."

"And what's the reason yer out here?"

"Searchin fer something," the boy answered quickly.

"Well. I can understand that, now I can." The man smiled at the boy and took a long drag on the cigarette and blew out some of the smoke from his nostrils. "Yeh got yerself a name?"

"Don't reckon names is that important anymore."

The man laughed heartily and then coughed. "Got a head on yer shoulders don't yeh?"

Josiah shrugged. He ran his finger through some of the grease that was left on the plate and stuck his finger in his mouth and then sucked the taste off of it.

"I'll tell yeh, son," the man said, "A name don't mean a thing when yer out in God's land. Everthin out there either knows yer name or don't care bout it. It ain't important when yer out there." He smiled a wide, toothy grin. "But come round people and civilization, that's when names are needed. That's why we're given them names in the first place."

Josiah nodded quietly. "What's yer name, then?"

"Walter Densen. Ain't that hard to own yer name, ceptin it's somethin yeh want to forget."

"Josiah Fuller."

"See," Densen said, leaning back in his chair. "Nice to meet yeh." He leaned forward again and brought the cigarette to his mouth and smoked. "Now, yer Josiah Fuller an yer searchin fer somethin that you ain't gonna tell. Yer a puzzle, boy. Yeh got yerself a gun, I suppose."

The boy nodded and waited for the man to continue, but he didn't. Instead, Densen sat without moving and smiled. He drew heavily on the cigarette and let drop some of the spent ash on the table and picked some of the stray shavings of tobacco from his tongue and lips and then took another draw.

The boy set the rifle on the table and pushed it across to the man before him. Without looking down at the gun, Densen reached out his gloved hands and felt around the table and found the gun and picked it up and felt it with his hands, his fingers running the length of the wood and pausing once and again on the cold metal. He fingered the trigger and then brought the object up to his nose and drew a deep breath in. "That's a nice piece, son." Densen smiled and handed it back to the boy. Josiah took it and set it down next to his chair and then leaned in toward the man across from him and saw that the man's eyes were clouded over, some strange milky lining resting over them, a grotesque veil. They were dead eyes to a world removed of life.

Josiah was quiet. He held his breath without realizing it, and the man smiled and took another draw on the cigarette and then laughed.

"Took yeh long enough, didn't it son."

"I didn't know," Josiah said.

"That's all right. I seen yeh come in earlier. Thought yeh could use a bit a help. Oh now, don't get me nothin wrong, boy. Jus cause I ain't got no workin eyes don't mean I cain't see. I can see jus fine. Ain't distracted by whatever else it be that yeh all see. I see what I gotta see and that is enough." Densen rubbed his right hand on his face. Then he continued: "Seein and knowin is about the same thing, Fuller, exceptin I'm talking bout my type of seein, not yers nor that world's out there about us. Yeh remember that one thing on yer quest of searchin whatever it is, son."

Josiah nodded his head.

"What all yeh want fer that gun there, boy?" The man turned his head toward the street, sensing some passing spirit out beyond the small room. He smiled and then he sniffed the air like a dog would.

"I ain't askin nothin fer it. And I ain't sellin it. Been in my family a while yet and I intend to keep it such."

"How bout forty? Forty United States dollars?" He drew forth from his pocket a small bundle that clanged on the table when he set it down. "Then again, it mightn be a bit more. Mighta miscounted." The man laughed again at his joke.

"I can't do that, sir. Obliged over the offer, but I ain't givin it up."

Densen smiled again. "Why yeh need a gun fer, son? What's the real thing yer after? Blood? Cause if it is, I can bout guarantee it that you'll find what yer after if that is what yer lookin fer deep down in that heart of yers. Blood's everwhere. Jus look about yeh. It's in here and it certainly is out there." Densen motioned with his head to the street outside. "But just you hear me here boy, vengeance and blood is a slippery ground. Yeh stand yerself up once and yer bound to fall right back down, jus the next time you'll fall a bit further and further yet til yeh can't bout stand yerself up any more. An a gun ain't much use fer anything else ceptin blood an ended life. So how bout I ask yeh again? Forty dollars. Take it and go on home or wherever such place it is yeh come from and leave the world as it be?"

"I can't. Ain't got no place to go."

Densen nodded. He took a long draw on the cigarette. The smoke lifted from the tip of the thing and Josiah watched as it disappeared just above Densen's head. "Unnerstood," the man said quietly. He scraped the coins from the table and replaced them in his pocket. "A nice piece of work like that one there is meant to be used and used well, I can tell yeh that. It might well bring yeh luck there on yer quest, though. Hope so fer yerself. Just hope it don't bring no bad falls to yeh, as some guns do to their holder. I was jus tryin to save yeh from doin something with that gun of yers you ain't meant to do."

Josiah nodded and then stood up to leave. He thanked the man and picked up the rifle and was turning to go to the front entrance when the man called out to him. "Set a little while more. Fer an old blind man's sake."

Josiah nodded and said all right and then sat back down.

"If I can't deter yeh from yer path, then may I offer a bit of help along yer way?"

"All right." Josiah's voice was still quiet, sounding afraid even.

"What is it yeh need to know?" The man stubbed out his cigarette on the table and then dropped the white paper remains on the floor next to his foot. He moved his gloved hand over the darkened table, letting his fingers play out some tune on an imagined piano, shuffling the air between the two of them.

The boy sat mute, staring at the gloves. He looked up to the man's face. It was still hidden in shadows. Densen seemed familiar to him, like he had met him once before in a dream that he had forgotten and only now called forth from his memory, but it was a memory that was blurred from reality and he did not know. "I'm trackin a rider," Josiah said. His voice had gained some heaviness to it.

Densen nodded.

"A rider in black."

"What color's the horse."

"Black."

"Like Death, huh?" The man chuckled. "Yeh sure yeh want to be trackin that rider?"

"It ain't Death. An I am."

The man sat. Under the shadows, his face contorted, twisting in thought. "I cain't say fer certain that I can recall such a man, but I will be keepin a steady ear out fer anything, though, and a mindful eye." Densen smiled and rolled another cigarette and then lit it with a match and then drew deep on the paper. He began to cough and spat a smoking wad of phlegm onto the floor and then turned back to the boy. "Let me ask yeh this, though: how yeh know yer goin the right way? Could be goin anywhere and yeh set out and believe it's right? Yeh can only hope it's right, yeah?"

Josiah looked at the man, quietly judging his face. Then he said: "I got me faith. Belief that I'll be led there."

"Belief in what, son? God?"

"Belief in the right thing." Josiah turned and looked at the gathering crowd in the small room behind him. "I thank yeh fer yer help, but I gotta be movin along."

The man nodded. "Why don't yeh stay a while with one them whores up the stairs there? Maybe forget bout this here adventure yer on, clear yer mind some boy? Ain't nothin a good time with one of them won't fix. Believe you me, I know."

"I gotta be goin."

"Son, yeh either must stop sayin yeh gotta be gone or get goin on yer way." He crushed the cigarette into the table and looked back up to the boy. "Let me tell yeh a story real quick like and then yeh can be gone. How's that settle wit yeh? One story."

"All right." The boy nodded and sat back in the chair.

"All right, then. The story goes like this: There was once a man, olden man, older than me even. An this man thinks he's cursed, thinks God and Satan that they're playin a trick on him. Calls hisself Job, liken the Bible. Goes round tellin everbody his name's Job—everbody there is to tell. Now don't yeh fret none, boy. I ain't bout to recycle none of scripture fer yeh. Ain't no nickel preacher man none. Ain't nothin but lies no such anyhow in that there Bible book. Pardon me if yeh believe in them lies, though. But yeh want to hear them then come on Sunday and you'll hear em all.

"Anyhow, this man Job, well, his wife is dead. Shot down one morning in her house that she shared with Job. Same as his two sons and three daughters. All shot in the head. Man says when he found em they was all lined up in a row, hands draped cross they chests like they was fixin fer a true Christian burial. All cept coins in they eyes. An this man Job, he had come home from the market or some such place as the story tells, an he finds em. Now, he screams an screams, cursin God and the devil, an he sets fire to that house of his what he built with his own two hands an his own sweat an blood, what he did slave hisself over for days and months an whatnot. An he sets fire to it an leaves. Becomes a wanderer in the hills, scratchin hisself raw and tearin his flesh an beatin his chest and callin out to God in spite an in hate.

"Well, this man finds hisself in town one day and sees another man bein led to the whippin post. This man Job, now, he asks what's this man's crime and comes to hear murder of a family on up the river, caught not three nights before fer it. And mind yeh, this ain't Job's family, but some other. And this man Job, comes to hear that he, this other man Job sees, is bein led to his end, whipped and flogged and beatin to death is his sentence they tell him. Horrible way to go out, boy. Horrible. Yeh feel yer life bein kicked out of yeh slow like until yeh cain't move but still yeh see and hear the sound of that leather smackin gainst yer bloody and torn body.

"But anyhow, our man Job believes hisself to be starin at the murderer of his family. Maybe the man is, maybe the man ain't—that ain't the point of this here story, son. But Job watches fer twenty some minutes as they tie this other man up and flog him with the strap of leather. Takes three different men to do him in. And the whole time, between each snap of the whip, this beatin man screams out. 'I couldn't help it,' he yells out to everone there, 'I couldn't help it.' Finally, they stop peltin him with the strap and leave his slumped carcass to rot in the middle of this here square they're in. An people, good men and women, Christian men and women, children even, come over and spit on this quiverin an nothin thing of a bein, disfiggered, lookin more like some rottin slab of beef than a man.

"Well this Job goes over and looks at this slump of a thing and grabs this thing's head, pryin open the eyes so as he can take a good look in his undoer's soul, so's he believes it.

"Little while later, as our man Job is walkin through the streets he overhears some gossipgagglin women talkin bout how this other man, now slumped dead in the streets, had a family of his own. An he listens to these women an they all of em talk bout this man, askin theyselves and wonderin and questionin why some people come to be like that. No answer they come to find, I reckon. Anyways, this man Job asks after this family, an he ain't have no luck atall finding information bout a dead man's past—some things I suppose get buried with yeh under the dark dirt of a grave.

"But Job now—he ain't bout to quit on the one thing he has left in this world—so he goes off in search of this dead man's family. An, believe you me if yeh can, he finds em not some month later all up in the mountain hills, far off from the town. What happened was this man, the dead one that is, had run off from that family. I reckon he hit his wife around and their daughter, age eleven, and sons—they was two of em. A family much like our man Job, now mind yeh. Well, anyhow, Job finds em in this house an one night walks into that place and slits they throats, ever last one of em, while they sleep. And he sits there after, dippin his hands in they blood and paintin his face like some heathen. They found the bodies some days after, rotted and pecked on by animals."

Josiah looked at the empty plate in front of him. "What happened to him?"

"Who? Job?"

The boy nodded. "Yeah."

Densen turned his head away from the boy. After several seconds he turned it back. Josiah thought he could see tears running down the man's cheeks. "Cain't say. Maybe he up an killed hisself after he come to unnerstand what he done? Don't know." He sighed. "One rumor from that story tells of how this man Job went into the woods an stayed there fer some time, beatin an cuttin hisself with rocks an pine needles over what he come to do. An some will tell yeh that this man ended his time out there by takin a rock and carvin out his eyes so's he wouldn't have to look at the world an what he done."

The two were quiet. The boy looking at the man, the man looking into the darkness that was his world.

After some time, Densen sat back in his seat and began to pack tobacco in some paper and roll another cigarette. "What yeh think of that there story, son?"

The boy shook his head. "What yeh aimin at with that?"

"Nothin. Thought it was an interestin story when I's heard it some time since. Thought it an apt story fer yeh."

"It a true story?" Josiah asked

"Cain't say fer certain, though I wouldn't doubt it. I tend not to doubt much anymore."

"That you in the story?"

"Cain't say fer certain it was. Just a story, son."

Densen lit the rolled cigarette. The light showed his face and then it was extinguished from sight again and he was returned back to the dark. "I suppose I take from it that all men have some kind of bloodshed written in their past. Ceptin most are sensed enough not to go actin on it. Them family in that story ain't have no bearin on the man and what he done. But, that is life, son, an most people will turn to God fore they turn to they own selves. Suppose that the truest fact in existence is that we become what we are most afraid of. In truth, I reckon that yeh can find God in violence, you can become him. But in that becomin yeh lose yerself—Who yeh are, who yeh were, and yeh become somethin new."

The blind man took a deep breath and let it out slowly. "I'll leave you with this one mention, son, somethin I've come to realize over my time—We are all ghosts of other men that've lived before us, an if yeh want to go an plunge yerself into that darkness, boy, then yeh just have to follow that path yer on and it'll eventually lead yeh to that place, since them men that came before yeh did jus the same. Ceptin I don't reckon much that any man wants to face what lies at the end of that path. I surely do not."

Densen shook his head slowly and then stood. His entire body was covered in shadow now. He took off the glove that had been covering his left hand and reached into his pocket and pulled forth a handful of coins and let them drop on the table. They rattled loud and then everything seemed quiet, quieter than before. "Take these, son."

The boy looked down at the table at the small pile of coins—some copper, some gold, some silver. Josiah looked at the man. "I can't take that."

Densen smiled. "Yeh already have taken it, son. Just from sittin here with me. It's yers." Then the man's face tightened and the smile left his face. "Trust you me, son. At the moment of realization, when yer mind fully is aware and acceptin of all that it once rejected, that moment when yeh turn from whatever law yeh once held to, son, that moment becomes yer last and you will be lost forever an turned into somethin so vile that yeh cain't even name it—yeh wouldn't want to." He shook his head, then continued: "If you write yer life around exactin some kind of revenge, it will destroy you, spiral out of yer power til yeh cain't control it, an it'll devolve into some monster beast that yeh cain't cage. Every person feels that, but most have sense enough to know not to chase no runaway vengeance. Remember that, son." The man turned his head and sniffed at the air. "Smells like snow'll be rollin in not too far away yet." And then he walked off, a limp in his step. His cane carefully clicked on the floor before him, searching his surrounds—a sight to an unseen world.

The earth is a chalk powder, its surface loose and turned a deep crimson color, seemingly stained as such from the constant battles fought over its time. Above this ground circle three birds. They are black and soundless, crows maybe, but they are too high above to tell for certain. These winged things glide smoothly against the blue and white of the sky, blackening the sun only for a moment before continuing on in their flight. To look at them, you would think that they were trapped in that world above us.

On this dry ground you can see the dark double of them, but still it is not the birds on the ground but rather mere reflections of them, stretched tightly against this world, testing the limits of what is and what is not. The shadows circle about, twisting and conjoining, sometimes separating, other times remaining as one. They move in some misplaced pattern that only nature knows, and not even the birds themselves know this pattern.

Cooper and Wilkins decided to stop for the night about a mile from the small mining camp. They had passed on the outer rim of it an hour or more before and had doubled back after a little while to get a better look at the place. There seemed to be only two or three dozen men and about that many small wooden shacks, as well. The two men watched as carts of black earth were hauled from the mineshafts, some pulled by horses and others by straining men, and loaded in a massive pile onto a large open spot of land that had been turned a permanent black by the coal.

The two men had left their post, planning to enter the mining camp the next morning and take what they could and leave quickly.

They had been slowly moving westward, hiking through the backhills of the country, and killing small rodents—gophers and squirrels—for food. They wanted to reach the state line by the time the winter storms began, when the ground would be covered in white.

Wilkins sat on the dirt and was removing the fur and skin from the bloodied animals he had killed not long before. He pulled the blade sharply through the animal in his bloodied hand, ripping the thin skin from the meat. He dropped the cut pieces at his side, where there was already a small collection of heads that he had already removed.

Cooper looked around the small clearing that they had stopped in and told Wilkins that he was setting off to collect wood for the fire and that when he returned they would cook the meat and eat. It had been a few days since either had eaten much and the thought of the roasted meat made them even more hungry. Wilkins didn't say anything but only nodded and dragged the small brown bag closer to where he sat and continued on as before.

Cooper set off in the direction they had come and then turned. He marked his location by carving lines with his knife in the trunks of the trees that he passed. After a while he came across a small stream and he bent down on his hands and knees and, like an animal, brought his lips to the water and slaked his thirst. The water was cold and stung his teeth and he had to spit out some of the water that he held in his mouth before swallowing. He dipped his cupped hands in the water and drank from them again. Beyond where he knelt was a small buck, its tethered antlers seemingly weighing the thing down. Cooper jumped up quickly and was going to throw his knife at the animal but the movement had spooked the buck and it ran off into the trees. He squinted but couldn't see where the animal had disappeared to. He shook his head and then looked to the ground. All of the branches and twigs were wet from the stream. He decided to move on further west of where he was to look for kindling and things to burn for the coming night.

The sun was setting fast overhead and it was not long before he found himself in darkness with only the moon and stars above him to show him any way at all. He had collected a good armload of wood and was about to head back to the camp when he heard the sound of a horse running. He set the wood at his feet and he listened closer and began to walk quickly in the direction of the sound. After a while, he came to the edge of a wide and open field and saw the house standing in purple silhouette to the night sky. There was a porch and a railed banister that circled the house, and in front of the house was a large field that looked like molasses in the dark. Not far from the house was a second, smaller structure that looked to be a barn, and attached to the back of the barn, all one building, was a horse stable. The only light Cooper could see from the whole area came from this second structure: the entrance to this place was lit from the inside by several lanterns that cast their spells out into the dark. The bigger house may have been lit from within as well, but Cooper couldn't tell—the drawn curtains and closed doors only seemed to add a quiet mystery to the house.

Cooper looked back over to the barn. At its entrance was the horse he had heard earlier, and standing next to the animal were two shadowed figures of men that stood and talked to each other quietly. These figures stayed this way for a minute or two before one of them turned and walked to the large house and the other took the reins of the horse and led it toward the small structure behind him.

Cooper turned from the field and began the journey back through the skeletal trees, back to Wilkins, to tell him of the discovery of the house and barn and the change of their plans.

And behind him, within seconds, the two figures, man and beast, disappeared in the barn and became absent from the land. The only things left were the two dark and looming structures in the open field and the soft tinker's glow coming from the barn.

She tells him quietly as they sit looking at the moon hanging high in the night.

"I'm with child," is all she can manage. There are tears in her eyes and she needs to wipe them away in order to see him. He doesn't say anything; instead, he puts his arms around her and brings her body close to his. She can feel his heart beating within his chest. Though she cannot see them, he too has tears in his eyes and the beginnings of a smile on his lips, and she knows this.

The boy slept in an actual bed that night. He had taken the coins that had been left on the table for him and put them in his pocket and then asked the barman where to go to get a room for the night and then went over to where the barman said. The boy received a key in return for a few of the coins.

Inside the room, Josiah slowly took off his boots and laid down his gun next to the bed and sat on the padded blankets and then lay back and looked up at the ceiling and closed his eyes and slept.

He didn't wake until late the following morning when the sun was already high. He was beginning to open his eyes, feeling rested for the first time in days, when one of the whores barged into the room and slammed the door behind her. Josiah sat up straight and grabbed for the gun that still lay next to him.

"Be quiet. Let me stay here fer a minute. Shhh," she said to him in a loud and angry whisper. She looked young to the boy, not much older than himself, if even. She was a plaything in harlequin; a deep rouge was spread on her harlot's cheeks, flush red, and there was thick eyeliner that circled about her eyes, as if guarding a pit from which there could be no counter, nor any return. There were streaks in the liner from where she had been crying, and her breath was quick and her body red and sweaty. She bent over, placing her hands on her knees and shook her head back and forth, the golden-red curls moving heavily this way and that.

She disgusted the boy in many ways, but at the same time he could think of nothing more than what the touch of her skin felt like, the taste of her bitter sandpaper tongue, the feel of her hot breath against his body, of flesh on his flesh. She stood up again and pressed her weight against the door, holding it tightly shut with her body, her hand clenched around the knob of the door, her hand turning white from the grip, her body small, her hand shaking, her face painted in terror, her face.

She looked back at Josiah, who had remained seated the while. He tried to stand from where he sat but he found that he couldn't. He could only watch her. "If anyone asks, yeh ain't seen me this mornin. Yeh hear me?"

Josiah was about to ask her name when she cracked open the door, looked out and, seeing that it was clear, moved quickly outside, slamming the door shut behind her. After several seconds of staring at the closed door he stood and put his boots on, grabbed his gun, and felt with his hand that the coins were still where they had been when he fell asleep the night before. Once satisfied, he walked out the door, dropped the keys off at the desk and walked outside to his horse. The boy didn't notice the girl from his room, nor did he hear her cries for help, nor see the older man who was beating her as he walked his horse out of the town.

William Corvin

When I was young I was told that it would someday fall to me. Never wanted it, though. I always thought it more of a hassle than a thing with any true benefit. And I hated him for it. But they could never understand it, my mother especially. She thought a good education was enough to set me on the right path and that the path was standin behind him. That's why I left, I think. I ran off when I was fifteen. Just still a boy, but I never saw myself as that then. I guess none of us see ourselves as we really are until later, when we can look back at ourselves from another time. I didn't bother much thinkin of him until I heard he died. I never heard of my mother dyin, though. I was told later that she died not long after I left home. But him, he died years after I left, and I only randomly heard it from some man in a shop one day on my way out to Bluff County. Looked over and heard this man tellin it to some other group of gathered men. ' Corvin Coal owner died last week,' he said, and they all talked about what was goin to happen with getting coal for their stores and homes. That's when I came to realize it all fell on me, whether I wanted it or not, whether I was there or not. It wasn't for another while after I heard about it, though, that I set back home with her. Maria. Six months after I heard that man I found her, or maybe she found me—can't be certain, but I reckon it was the latter . . . I rode back home with her next to me, back to the life I wanted so badly to leave behind and forget. And we were married in the church after we returned back home . . . It wasn't til I got home again and started the mines up and settled the problems with the bank that I realized how lucky I was that I never got caught nor strung up neither. I should have; I realize that now. I've seen many men hanged by the neck til dead, and I've heard many people in the crowd say 'That's what he gets for livin some fool crazy life like he did.' But I didn't. I can only guess I'm jus lucky, or blessed, and I don't know why.. I don't know if there's much a difference between them two, bein lucky or blessed . . . I never did what I did for a life like that. I just wanted a life that didn't come from money and education with them tutors and schoolbooks. I hated it all. I wanted a life like I heard from my grandfather—my father's father that is—before he started the mines. I wanted the kind of life I read about in stories. I wanted to spare myself of my father's kind of life, the one you get born into with no say so yes or no. And I wanted to be rid of him an the way he would look at me an talk to me, like I was nothin but a waste to him. But you can't always outrun your fate. That fate will come back and haunt you, follow you like a stray, and when you turn to look on it, that's when it'll go ahead and bite the legs you thought you had under you. And that's how I think of it now.

6

There was no moon above him and The Rider was forced to light matches so that he could see where he was walking. He would strike one and let the flame burn down until it reached his fingers and then he would shake the small glow away and let the spent wood of the match fall to the ground before lighting another one. Behind him he could hear the horse's footsteps back and forth on ground and the quiet and steady sound of it eating from the dried grains and grasses of the earth. Those seemed the only sounds to his world.

The Rider found a small formation of rocks set against the dark night. A sacramental stone cathedral that in the night was clothed in some unknown superstition. The Rider laid his blanket on the ground next to the rocks and kneeled down. He set fire from one of the matches to a small lantern, the wick of which was almost extinguished. The dancing light was weak and barely reached the area surrounding the lantern.

The Rider pulled the knife from the scabbard that was hanging from his belt and undid the small bag that he held tightly in his hand and lay it on the ground before him. The bag was now dried and crusted. With the knife he began to scratch away the needles and twigs and dust that covered the ground, and then he began to dig away chunks of the earth, cutting the floor of the world with the blade. He moved the loose dirt aside until he had a small hole some ten inches deep. He put the knife down and then picked up the small bag and emptied its contents on the ground in front of him. Pieces of flesh—ears and strips of skin, a nose and a few tips of what had been fingers, and four eyeballs—now merely shriveled scabs of what was. The Rider arranged the dismembered parts neatly before him and they seemed to be the fossils of some ancient race now removed from the world and removed from the memory of man. And The Rider, as he knelt before these things, seemed a man merely studying these fossils in search of what had preceded him, hoping that in knowing them he would come to know himself. What had they been? And who was he?

Slowly, The Rider picked up each piece and dusted it off, rubbing hard with his own blackened fingers on the hardened and dry skin of these things, and then he gently lay each within the hole before him. His eyes were closed and he whispered inaudible words to himself. His body swayed gently from side to side and after he had finished the burial he slowly covered the hole over with the loose dirt and packed it tight. Salty tears fell on the mound before him and he whispered quietly aloud, "Now you are free." And then he blew the lantern flame away and then moved over by where the horse still ate and lay on the ground, the sepulchre only steps away. He closed his eyes, which still stung with the tears, and let sleep overcome him. "Amen."

Josiah had collected several armloads of kindling and had set aflame these pieces of brush and tree and earth. The blaze reached into the night sky, the tongues of the fire scattering in each direction. The boy lay back on the hard ground and shivered. The day before had been colder than he had felt yet on his journey, and the night was colder still. He wrapped himself in the blanket and thought of the whore from the hotel. He saw her face close to his, her hands gently caressing his arms and stomach, her hands sliding his pants down, fingers running the length of his legs, and then the feel of her mouth on him. His body shivered.

When he opened his eyes again he saw that the fire was just coals and embers barely alight and he fed more branches to the darkening pit and before long the flames began their process of stretching toward the sky and disappearing just as quickly as they rose only to be followed behind by more flames. The boy closed his eyes and fell asleep again, his face feeling the warmth from the fire.

The flames cast demon shapes upon the surrounds of the small area that the boy inhabited. The shadowplay performed on the branches of the night. Otherworldly beings were birthed in that light, within the dust and the trees. They made the shapes of animals on the walls of the world. Grotesque and distorted and skittering figures that did not exist, save in the imaginings of children, were created in the nighttime. They were solitary beings left alone in their unnatural communion, separated from the rest of mankind, and in them was created a new species that dissolved in the passing of night to day.

When the boy woke again it was morning and he could hear birds in the trees above him. The sun was not yet up and there was a heavy fog that seemed to be settled over the earth. He sat upright and began to roll the blanket that he had spread over his shivering body the night before when he saw a black smoke rising through the fog, above the trees. He let drop his hold of the blanket and grabbed his gun. He turned to the horse and quieted the animal and then he walked in the direction of the smoke. His face began to sweat in the cool of the morning.

After a while, the boy came to a small hill that was covered in rocks and some low hanging trees and he trudged up it carefully, his eyes continuously roaming about him. As he came near the top of the hill, he lay on his belly and shuffle-crawled his way forward so that he could look down at whatever it was that was burning. He hid himself behind a rock and peered out. Below him he could see two men sitting next to a campfire. The smoke was a deep black that seemed to bellow from within the earth and escape into the air. A putrescent odor came from below him and the boy saw one of the men eating the meat of some small animal. The other man was turned away from both the fire and his companion; this man had a bag open and was laying on the ground what looked like blackened sticks, six or seven in number, ranging from five or so inches to ten. Both men wore heavy coats that had once been a brown but now looked black, and one of them wore a haggard looking confederate hat. Holes decorated their coats and pants, and the boots on their feet looked torn and used.

"Watch yerself, Wilkins," the first said, throwing the rest of the meat piece into the flames before him. "Don't be settin none of that off here."

The other man looked up and then began to replace the black sticks into the bag. "All right, then," Wilkins said.

"Remember. Jus like I showed yeh yesterday. Put em right there where I told yeh: two in the mine cave and two more next to them shacks. Light em an run. I'll put the others on the other side an we'll meet up at the house. All right?"

Wilkins nodded.

The boy's eyes drifted back and forth on the land before him. He couldn't see any other men, nor could he see any horses or animals that these drifters could be using. To the east, some three or four miles off, the sky was covered in low clouds so that you could hardly see the hillsides of the valley on either side. When the boy looked back to the men he saw that they had stood and were kicking dirt on the fire pit.

Josiah began to back away from the edge of the hill, away from the rock. He turned and walked back to his own camp to gather his horse and blankets. Behind him he could hear the men still talking. One of them said to the other: "We ain't too far off yet." The boy turned back to the hill once more but the smoke was now cleared from the air as if it had never actually existed and had only been in the boy's mind the whole time.

Corvin woke in the middle of the night before. He had lay in his bed in the dark of the room, looking at the ceiling, trying to decipher the shapes of things known and unknown that seemed to float before his eyes. He could feel the warmth of Maria beside him. And he lay like this, content within the dark hours of the night that seemed without end, and he would have had it remain that way, just so, until the end of time.

He had fallen back asleep and now woke again, sleeping later than he normally did. He looked at his pocket watch that he kept on the table beside the bed and saw that it was nearly ten. He dressed himself quickly and walked out of the house.

Outside was a thick layer of fog. The man stood on the porch of the house, looking out at the gray, low cloud that seemed to intrude upon him and the house, swallowing everything in its way. It was a creature entity entirely its own—calculating, forever present, watchful and judging. The man walked down the steps toward the barn. "Jefferson," he called out.

Jefferson came from the fog, a phantom figure in the late morning. "Yessir," he said.

"Get my horse saddled."

Jefferson nodded and then looked behind the man. "Missus ain't joinin yeh today neither?"

Corvin shook his head. "Lettin her sleep." He looked back to the house and then said quietly, "I'm to be a father, Jefferson."

The negro smiled and then turned and went inside the barn and on to the stable to saddle the horse. After a few minutes, Jefferson led the horse out into the cool morning, the water in the air clinging to the horse's hairs.

Corvin smiled and began to climb up to the saddle when he stopped and his chest felt heavy and empty, his stomach hurt. A thunderous cracking and rumbling sound erupted in the distance. Then there were several smaller explosions that broke through the quiet of the place. The ground beneath the two men shook and Corvin quickly looked out at the distance and then down at Jefferson. Jefferson looked up at the man, his face featureless.

"My God," Corvin said quietly, whispering it under his breath and to no one in particular. He turned the horse and began to ride at a near gallop in the direction of the mining camp; over his shoulder he called out to Jefferson something that Jefferson couldn't hear—he was too far away, swallowed now by the fog entirely.

The Rider sat his horse a few yards away from the empty campsite. He walked slowly toward the fire pit and knelt down and placed his hands over the blackened logs and scraps of wood that had once been alight. They were cool to his hand with only the faint hint of a past heat. He guessed that the owner of this camp and the flames that had settled here had left the area a few hours before. Beside the fire pit were the drying carcasses of several small animals; flies were already landing gently on the sinewy skin.

He stood and tried to peer through the fog, but he could see nothing and he could hear nothing. It had become thicker and darker in the few hours he had been awake, and the fog now created a barrier that seemed impenetrable, a prison of the world's own making.

Behind him was a hill covered in rocks and a few short trees and he began to circle the hill from behind and climb up it. When he reached the peak of the hill he looked down and could see the fire pit and he could see his horse eating grasses and plants and he looked out, scanning the horizon. The fog seemed to stretch to the ends of the earth and even beyond, a dark and phantasmal creation clinging to the ground for sustenance. The Rider could see the tops of the trees breaking through the thick black and gray layer of the cloud. Most of the trees were bare, with only ancient and arthritic fingers pointing upward, but there were still some colored leaves, red and yellow and orange, which shone like semaphores heralding the return of fallen soldiers.

He turned around and looked out upon the southern land and studied the dirt and trees and plants that stretched before him. He felt as if he were surveying a landscape from another time altogether. And as he looked out at this place, void of man, he wondered what was to become of this land and what was to become of himself, and he called out something primordial in itself that seemed to originate in the bowels of his body and dominate over the land: a call that reached to the furthest regions of space, reaching a high crescendo before dropping off as easily as it began, like ripples in a vast ocean ceasing themselves of their wayward trance and allowing life to rest quietly once again until the next of the never-ending storms of time.

The Rider took a deep breath and began to walk down the hill. As he neared the bottom of the small hill he heard several loud explosions that echoed throughout the trees. Birds took flight above him, crying out loudly in the morning, and disappearing in the fog. The earth shook steadily under his feet only to rest quietly once again moments later, as if nothing had happened.

When Josiah heard the steady roll of the explosions he had just entered a large, wet meadow field. Birds called out loudly and flew from their perches to some other region of the world, away from the rolling echoes of the sound.

This field was vacant, surrounded only by dense thickets of birch and cedars turned yellow and red in the late season. The grass there was turned a burnt color and the wet earth below seemed to give way under each of the horse's steps, as if it were journeying through quicksand. The fog seemed to grow more dense in this place and he felt himself lost from within, separated from the world even more so than before. Josiah thought that in the thick layer of smoky fog he could see the phantom ghosts of past warring men still battling, still clinging to the dirt and mud of this world, still remaining in this time although they had passed on to some other plain and were not meant to be here.

The air erupted in sound and the ground jarred below the horse's feet and the boy could only tell of the shaking ground from the collections of water scattered throughout the bog: small ripples that stretched from the center outward, becoming bigger and bigger. Then, from beyond the mist and after the sound of the explosions had disappeared in the quiet of the place, the boy heard a more thundering sound. A steady drumming. Louder than anything before. Josiah reached for the rifle at his side and brought it up to his face, resting the gun calmly against his shoulder and his cheek. He sat high on the horse, looking beyond the barrel to whatever creature it was that headed his way.

Through the thick, gray screen before him, he could see dark shapes passing quickly in the morning. He strained his eyes to see, but the shadows were moving too fast and the fog was still too dark. It looked to be deer or some other beast, he could not tell. He let the gun slip from where he held it and he watched the fleeing creatures for an answer to what they were. The rapid and steady percussion of feet running through and over the watery earth sounded and filled the meadow field.

He backed the horse a few steps, his eyes never leaving the misty wall before him, nor the dark animals that stampeded just past his view. And the whole while he wondered what it must be like to travel at such speed, such precision over the earth, without care, without hatred, without loss or pain or understanding.

Cooper and Wilkins ran through the trees and rocks and bushes of the woods, their arms stretched before them, bracing for some obstacle they could not see through the fog. After a while they slowed their pace and after a bit more time they stopped completely. They both doubled over from the run, their hands on their knees, out of breath; short phlegm-filled coughs came from their throats and they spat on the ground. As he caught his breath, Wilkins began to laugh and then cough. "Goddamn," he wheezed. "Them sticks blew that cave to piles."

"Shut up," Cooper told Wilkins. "We gotta git to that house fore he come back."

"You reckon he's there yet?"

Cooper looked back at Wilkins and then began to walk quickly through the trees toward the house. "Let's go," he called back. Wilkins followed closely behind, slinging the weightless bag higher onto his shoulder.

After a while, they could see the break in the trees and, even with the fog, they could see the house and barn stretching high above them. They stopped and Wilkins unslung the bag and set it on the ground. Cooper reached inside and pulled out a rusted gun and checked to make sure that it held bullets. He stuck it in the waist of his pants and then looked over at Wilkins. The latter was smiling goofily.

"Knock yer dumbed-assed grinnin off, boy. Jest like we talked bout, all right? There's jus the one in the barn. I'll take care of him and I'll git the horses ready. Alls yeh gotta do's go in the house there and git as much as yeh can find and fill that bag and then come out. No more, all right? You jus be quiet enough in there and don't wake no one else that might be there. I ain't seen no one else up at this time in the morning cept them two, the man and the nigger."

Wilkins nodded.

"All right, then. Let's go."

Wilkins headed quietly for the house as Cooper ran over the wet ground to the barn. As he neared the barn, he took the gun from his waist and held it aright, out in front of him. He stopped outside of the barn's open doors and peered quietly into the darkness. He could hear animals eating and near the back of the barn he could hear a scraping sound of metal and then the sound of footsteps from the man inside. Cooper turned back and saw Wilkins enter the house and then he peered around the edge of the door and into the barn again. He could see the black man walking toward him, a bucket in his hands, his head hanging down.

Jefferson walked toward the entrance of the barn and looked out past the yard, toward the trees that surrounded the place. Hidden there, he thought he saw a string of lights stretching off into the distance, and he wondered if they were from lanterns of travelers who had lost their way. He stopped and smiled briefly and then continued outside into the moist air. As he did so, Cooper leveled the gun at the negro's head and pulled the trigger. Jefferson's body jolted sideways. Blood sprayed the air as the bullet passed through him. Cooper looked at the body that was now slumped in a pile on the ground. The bucket that had been full of milk now lay on its side, the milk collecting in a pool and mixing with the blood and with the dust and dirt from the earth. Cooper knelt down and removed the boots from Jefferson's feet and fit them on his own and then stepped carefully over the body and into the barn toward the stable in the back.

Inside the house, Wilkins quietly crept through the front halls and into the dining room. The rooms were dark and he had to rub his eyes to see anything. He found a wooden box filled with silver forks and spoons and knives and he placed the box in his bag and then he continued on through the house, quickly taking random pieces of metal and wood that he imagined might be of worth. As he was halfway up the stairs, he heard the gunshot from outside. He stopped and looked in its direction, wondering whether he should continue on or leave. Then, from above him, he heard the heavy sound of footsteps on the wooden floor. He began to turn to go back down the stairs when the sound of the footsteps grew louder and closer, right above him.

Wilkins crouched against the side of the wall, gripping the bag tightly to his chest, holding to the shadows that lined the walls. He held his breath. Sweat began to bead on his forehead and it ran down his nose and cheeks. Wilkins looked to the top of the stairs and saw the silhouette of a woman hurrying quickly down the steps. His heart beat hard in his chest.

As the woman was two steps from him, he swung the near full bag at the figure and heard the heavy sound of the contents hitting flesh. The woman fell back, hitting her head on the steps and thumping down several steps before coming to a rest just below where he was standing. He cursed himself under his breath and looked around the room, waiting for someone else to come running to the woman's aid. After a few seconds, he ran down the stairs, carefully stepping over the woman. He looked down at her and saw her body sprawled over the steps in some unnatural geometric shape, her thick hair framed around her head in a black halo, and blood came from her head and what looked to be from her stomach area.

Wilkins cursed again and then ran out of the house, slamming the door hard behind him. Outside, Cooper sat on a brown and black spotted horse and in his hand he held the reins to another horse that sat on the far side of him. Wilkins slung the bag over his shoulder, grabbed the reins, and sat himself quickly on the saddle and rode off before Cooper could say anything to him.

A copper smoke continues to spew from the hillside. You can see it clearly, even with the dense fog of the day. Part of the smoke drifts to the sky and becomes lost in the wind while another part of it remains tethered to the land, and Corvin must ride through this smoke to enter the mining camp. Small fires have broken out in several places around the camp; flames stretch up the warped tree trunks and consume some of the small wooden shacks.

Different men call out to others who are running back and forth through the camp between the different caverns in the hillside. Some men frantically carry buckets of water from the surrounding streams while others haul tools and equipment—picks, axes, shovels. The men's voices bleed together and you cannot tell one from the other. And there is chaos all around.

Corvin quickly dismounts from the horse and runs to the western entrance of the mines that dig into the hillside. Several men, their faces turned a soot black, are laying on the hard, dark ground. Some wipe blood from one another's faces, some from their own. Behind these men are the now hollowed foundations of where their shacks once stood. Flaking pieces of wood and metal twisted from the blast lay scattered about the wet ground. Cotton stuffing from the bunks and clothes of the men are tossed here and there and there is no pattern to where these things now rest. The dark and bloodied men look up and watch as Corvin passes them. In the distance, a primal voice cries out and it is hard to tell if it is from pain or anger or some other emotion.

Nearer to the western entrance, Corvin meets up with another man. This man is gaunt. His arms and legs so thin that you might miss them if you look quick enough. A thick beard stretches down his neck and a thin streak of blood runs from an open cut on his forehead. "Boss," this man says.

"What happened?" Corvin asks.

"Figure its dynamite. Some number of sticks, I reckon. One or two placed over there near the bunk cabins, another two or three thrown down into this shaft, and over there, too."

"The other cave shafts?"

"Some cave in, I reckon. Haven't had the frame a mind to go inspect em all yet. Ain't no one hurt beyond the scratch and cut, though, thank God. Happened when we was all at breakfast, not started the first shifts of the day yet. Good fortune, I suppose, if we can call it that."

"One of the men do this, you think?" Corvin's eyes search the area slowly. He tries to take in the scene, but he can't bring himself to understand it yet.

"I don't reckon."

"Well." Corvin nods his head slowly. "Find out. This doesn't happen here. This doesn't. It can't." His voice rings through the camp, and several men near the two of them turn and watch. After some minutes, a boy of eighteen or nineteen walks up to the two slowly.

"Scuse me, Mr. Corvin . . ." He turns and looks at the boy. "Virgil there seen two men runnin off through the trees there jus fore the blast. You can ask him yerself if you like. Thought you might liken to know. Virgil say they was all dressed in rag clothes all torn an such an one a them had a sack slung over his shoulder. Least that's what he been sayin to anyone close nuff to listen to him."

Corvin nods. "All right, then." He turns to the gaunt man and wipes his face. The cold stings his fingers still. "Put these fires out, and start movin those rocks out to clear way for the shafts. This doesn't stop our production. Not now. We'd be done in if it did."

The gaunt man nods back to Corvin and then turns and moves away quickly. And it is at this moment, as Corvin's breath catches slightly in his chest, that he realizes what he is turning into.

It is the truest fact in existence: we become what we are most afraid of.

Josiah sat on his horse on the top of the hill. His eyes scanned the horizon as he quietly contemplated which direction to go next. In the distance he saw two horses riding quickly across the open space, a trail of dust kicking up behind the heavy footfalls. The boy's chest began to strain and his heart beat hard in his chest when he saw them, but when he looked more intently at the horses he saw that neither of them were black. And he watched them until he could no longer see them.

Josiah looked behind him, at the land from which he had come, and then he turned forward and watched the horses disappear into the haze of the land, and then he set forth again, not riding in any one direction but seemingly in every direction toward the end that he told himself he would eventually come to.

Corvin walked the horse slowly over the ridge and over to the barn and stable. As the two neared the barn, the horse began to shy away and Corvin had to pull hard on the reins to keep the horse moving forward. His feet dug into the dirt when he pulled. Everything seemed too quiet to him then, as if the animals and the wind itself knew of something that he did not—something that they did not want to speak of. The fog had finally blown away and the day was now turning black in the sky. He looked up and over to the house as he neared the barn and it wasn't until he looked back down to the ground that he saw Jefferson's body.

He let go of the reins and ran over to where Jefferson's body lay. Corvin nearly stumbled to the ground. The body had become stiff and cold since it first fell; flies flew around the head, some of them stopping and landing for a short second in the crater that had been carved out of the far side. Corvin knelt in the dust, now stained a black from the spilled blood, but he did not notice this. In the approaching dark, the entirety of the ground looked black and you could not tell one spot from the next and Jefferson's spilled blood only seemed to become one with the blood that had been spilled centuries before in unaccounted histories on this land.

Corvin's hands shook and his chest felt heavy and he breathed as if his lungs were absent of air, pulling in the oxygen in long and loud gasps. He rolled Jefferson's body over so that the negro's face shown up to the sky and then he ran over to the horse and grabbed a blanket from his pack and spread it over the dead man's body. Corvin stood then and quickly ran to the house, his eyes stained with tears and his heart beating hard in his chest, his temples throbbing in his head, and the air cold on his sweaty arms.

The door echoed loudly throughout the dark house as he threw it open. He called out Maria's name and waited for an answer, but the answer did not come back to him and he was only left in silence. He called again as he walked over to the kitchen area and then to the dining room. She was not there but he continued to call out. His voice broke in his strained call. He circled back to where he began and then walked over to the left of the house to mount the stairs to the second floor, and that was when he found her.

She was sitting on one of the bottom steps, her head bowed forward in some ghastly pose of prayer, her arms dangling between her legs. Surrounding her feet was a pool of dark liquid that the man didn't see until he knelt down and felt the coolness of it soak his knee. Placing his fingertips into the puddle and then bringing them to his nose, he smelled the familiar metallic odor; then he lifted her head and looked at the blank face, the eyelids closed in an exhausted sleep. He patted her face gently and then harder; her body fell slightly and he had to hold her steady. He tried to call her name, to ask her to wake, to rouse her, to yell to her, to scream, but he could say nothing. Finally, he picked her up and carried her to the dining room and laid her on the table and then fetched some matches and lit the candles on the table.

The room turned an antiquated and pale bronze in the candles' glow. He looked at his wife, her body spread flat on the table and saw the dark red stains on her dress skirt and the dried dark liquid that colored the length of her legs. His breath caught in his chest and he began to sob. He turned away from his wife and screamed out, his throat feeling as if it were being slashed by pieces of glass and dirt. The scream returned, only diminished now, in its echo through the lonely house. He turned back to Maria, his eyes and face a deep red now. He bent and rested his head down gently on her chest. He kept it there for several seconds before he could feel the faint lift and returned lowering of his head. The rise and fall of her chest as she breathed.

William Corvin

When I was a kid I used to sit under the trees on the hill an watch the trains come in. Every day I would go there. The earth would shake for some time before it came and then I would hear the engine and in the distance I would see the steam risin into the air to join with other clouds of white. Sometimes I would see some of the older boys get on the train and ride it to wherever they were called to go to first, all dressed in their blue uniforms, their rifles slinged over their shoulders and bayonets reachin to the sky—their mothers and their girls all cryin as the boys left on the train. But I was too young, they said to me, and all I could do was watch them go and imagine how they felt—scared and excited, I reckon most. I would sit there, sometimes hours at a time, not wantin to return home but wishin that I was somewhere else. Wishin I could run over to that train and climb up its metal sides and stow myself away or become one of them soldiers, and after countless stops further up that road on them tracks I would climb off and find a new life. But I couldn't. I was always too scared to. There wasn't anythin to keep me at home, though. That wasn't it. There was my father watchin me every day, frustrated with me always, hatin me for bein who I was, and my mother was always too scared to speak up and say a true thing to him. And there was me, lost in the middle of a world I never asked to be part of. I would read in the stories how men were supposed to be. I would follow their adventures along and wish I could be like them. But I could never get up from that spot under that tree. I could never take a step further to that train down there. It was always the same, but the fear of becomin him some day was enough to keep me goin there to that hill every day and watchin those trains come in and then sail away from me as I looked on and dreamed. It wasn't till I was fifteen that I found the courage, though. Wasn't my courage, though. It finally came to me after I sat with Jefferson. He was the only black man that my father allowed inside the house. There was the women cooks and cleaners, but no men. He was twenty some years older than me and had already buried his wife and two daughters before he came and talked to me that one day. Their bodies lay under a tree in one of the small clearings not far from the house. I remember how sad he looked when he came and sat next to me that mornin. Never had I truly talked to him before that day, but not a day passes yet that I don't think back and remember him and the way he came and sat next to me on the hill under the tree that day in the autumn after the leaves had fallen from their branches. He came over and sat down next to me and patted me gentle on the back and then said to me, 'They's two things I come to realize in my life. The first is that people don't live happily ever after none; they just live. An the second is that regret is an old man's burden, and you don't want that none, neither, not now and not when you do grow old.' I told him I didn't understand and he just smiled and handed me a handful of coins that he had been savin up and told me to go out there and find myself in the world before I became lost from it, and then he left me sittin there alone, lookin at the train comin in. And it was then, in that moment that seems an eternity ago, that I decided to leave everythin behind and go . . . I rode that train for nearly a day, knowin as I rode that the thing that was carryin me away from my life was bein powered by the very thing that I was escapin from. And I sat in that train car, watchin out the open door as the different lands passed me by in blurs of colors and shapes that seemed to be meltin before my eyes. And I would watch as trees passed and animals passed and I can remember how the train went next to a harvest field that was set ablaze and how the sky was a cloud of black. I would have guessed that anyone watchin the train from behind would have said that we were headed straight into the smoke and the fire and the ash and that we wouldn't be comin back out again.

7

The doctor, an ancient man with a thick white beard, shut the door quietly behind him and stepped out into the middle of the room to meet Corvin. The doctor's shoes clicked and echoed around the empty room, a dull, empty sound. It was the first sound that Corvin had heard in hours—the doctor had come in the house and entered the small room where Maria lay, turning to Corvin only long enough to tell him to stay outside the room.

The doctor walked over to Corvin set his brown leather bag at his feet and then took off his glasses and polished them with his shirt sleeve. Corvin waited cautiously, fearing whatever news the doctor would tell. Finally, the old doctor replaced his glasses on his nose and cleared his throat.

"Your wife lost the child. I'm sorry for that, William. I am. But the good news—what we all need to focus on now—is that she should recover in complete. Her pelvic bone, from what I can feel, is fractured and there's some damage to her ribs. She also has a heavy bruise on her head from where she fell and hit it that we still need to keep attention on for some time. But, given time, everything should heal completely."

Corvin nodded his head slowly. His eyes were filling with tears and he turned from the old doctor and wiped them away. His jaw trembled and he clenched his fist tightly in order to keep the rest of his body still.

The doctor continued: "She needs rest, William. Do you understand?"

Corvin turned back to face the doctor. He didn't say anything, nor did he seem to notice the small hermit of a man before him.

His eyes were lost in the recesses of the dark room.

"William?"

Finally, Corvin looked down at the doctor and nodded his head and then asked if he could see his wife. The doctor said he could, but not to wake her from her sleep.

Corvin opened the door slowly, afraid that any sound might wake her. He walked over to where she lay and stood above her, looking down at her sweating body. Then he knelt beside the bed. Maria's face was turned away from him. Droplets of sweat broke from her face and along her neck and he gently ran his fingers through her dark hair and then wiped the sweat from her forehead and then wiped the sweat from his hand on his pants. He leaned forward and kissed her forehead. He whispered something quietly to her and then turned and left the room. He walked past the doctor and out the door, grabbing hold of a glowing lantern and leaving the room behind him in dark. His quick steps sounded like bullet shots through the quiet of the place.

The morning was still black above him. He looked up and took a deep breath. The cold air seemed to cut through him and his fingers tightened and his breath became a fog. Along the distance of the horizon the sky was lightening to a blue, starting as a dark shade that would in time grow lighter and lighter. He could hear the heavy drone of the insects in the trees around him, a steady and comforting sound to him. He could also hear the sound of birds lighting from one branch to another and the heavy scuttle of predator and prey within the wooded lands that surrounded him. He thought of how their constant game with one another was an ancient one that had existed even before the olden times, in the days that preexisted the birth of man.

He walked into the barn, stepping carefully over where Jefferson's blood had been spilled. Many of the tools that decorated the walls of the barn had been stripped of their places by the intruders from the day previous; some of the tools lay scattered on the ground and others were missing entirely. The air inside the barn was stale and infested with the specks of dust that showed clearly in the light from the lantern that consumed the place and filtered out through the wood slats surrounding him.

Corvin walked to the farthest corner of the place and knelt. He pried the floorboard with his shaking hands, now turning a pale blue in the cold. From beneath the floor he removed a shortbarreled rifle and a pistol. He stood, not bothering to replace the board, and then walked over to one of the two remaining horses, the pale brown horse that he had ridden to the mining camp the day before. On its hind leg was branded the initials W.C. and he touched the initials softly, running his hand over the animal. He saddled the horse, packing a sack with blankets and some food, then he checked that the rifle and pistol were loaded and then walked the horse out into the yard.

Corvin was climbing onto the horse when he heard the front door of the house open and shut and he looked over and saw the aged doctor walking over to where he and the horse were.

The doctor looked up at the man. "Whatever it is you're thinking of doing, I'm asking you to put it away from your mind. Enough's already happened here. Enough damage. Don't add to it, William. Please."

He looked down at the doctor. His eyes were red and there were still tears running down his cheeks. His jaw tightened as he gripped the leather reins with his numb hands. "I can't do that."

The doctor looked around the empty yard and pulled his coat around him tighter in the cold. "It takes one act, William. One act of contradiction, one act of opposition to a person's belief, that's it. That one act is all you need. You hear me, son? Your mind accepts it and then it starts to want it, hunger for it, and then that's all that's left of you. Do you understand what I'm saying? This is that act, what you're about to go off and do. This is it."

Corvin shook his head from side to side and then he turned the horse.

"Don't go back to who you were, William. Not when you've come so far from that person."

He looked down at the old man and shook his head. "I can't

give it up," he said.

The doctor walked over and placed his hand gently on Corvin's leg and looked up at the man. "Life is all about answering for the mistakes of the past, repenting them, William, and in some way you can seek atonement for them. If you go out there today, then you are giving in to it. If you go out and do this, then you will be lost completely. I can promise you that."

Corvin walked the horse forward so that the doctor's hand fell away from its hold on his leg. He turned in his saddle and looked at the house and the barn and the old doctor standing alone in the field. "Make sure to keep her safe. Do whatever you have to. And see that Jefferson gets a right burial in the family yard. Next to her."

"Who?" the doctor asked.

"His wife." Corvin turned and faced forward, back out into the wilderness in front of him. In that moment, he felt torn, so distant from the world that he was riding out into and so removed from the one he was leaving behind. And he remembered Maria as she lay in the bed—she seemed so peaceful, but he knew she would wake and she would hold her empty belly and he did not know what he would be able to tell her. He brushed a cold tear from his cheek and then he dug his heels into the horse and the two set off, striking from this land of comfort and into some unknown one of vengeance, traveling a road that has been journeyed by so many men before him.

His breathing was shallow, coming in short, strained gasps in the cold morning air. His body twitched and his hands moved violently as if they were being attacked with spasms over and over again.

He woke quietly and found himself seated in the center of a small clearing; he could see no paths to lead him to or away from where he was and he could not remember how he had arrived there. Sweat was on his arms and the back of his neck, and his body shook. He stood and walked over to the black horse and pulled down another blanket that he had been using to keep the horse warm and he wrapped it around himself and then walked with the horse over to where he had been sleeping and picked up some of the dried fruit that he had eaten the night before and fed them to the horse. The Rider knelt down and set fire to some pieces of kindling and wood that he had collected the previous night and sat next to it, letting the fire warm his cold arms and legs. As he looked into the growing flames he remembered the dream that he had woken from:

The angel from his youth had come to him again, but she didn't say anything, even when he begged her to speak. Instead, she turned from him and began to leave him, walking in the other direction, leaving him behind. And he remembered how he was kneeling on the hard, dry ground while worms and insects crawled about his hands and his knees. He tried to rise from where he was, to stand and run to where the angel was at, he wanted to catch her and hold onto her, pull her back to him, but he couldn't. He couldn't stand, he couldn't move, even. He could only watch her walk away from him as the insects began to climb onto his hands and up his arms and legs and begin to bite his skin, and he cried tears that only fell on the ground and on the insects and he looked down at them.

Then he heard a gunshot, loud in the small area, and he looked up to where the angel was. Her body was now laying on the ground; the light that had surrounded her was now gone, and in her place there stood a boy of eighteen or nineteen, but he could not see the boy's face because of the shadows, and behind the boy he thought he could see another man, one with skin rotted or melting, flames seeming to rise behind him, and what looked to be a sword on fire in this man's hand. And The Rider looked to the sky and saw that the sun was being covered by dark clouds and that the sky was beginning to storm and that rain and snow were now falling, and then he looked to the boy and saw him walking closer to where he knelt, his body now being entirely consumed by the insects, and he could hear in the distance the sound of wolves baying at the sky and the calls of birds he would no longer know, and the boy took a pistol from his belt and pointed it at The Rider and pulled the trigger. And then he woke up.

The Rider's chest hurt him and he felt tears growing in his eyes and he brushed them away with his hands. He pulled the blanket around him more tightly now as he sat before the fire. He looked about him, around the small clearing, looking for some semblance of life or of death, but he found none. He was alone.

It was not long after the sun had come up fully and had warmed the dusty ground that Corvin came upon an ancient well made of dark granite stones smoothed over from the wind and time and the other perpetual forces of this world. The only texture that the stones seemed to have was from the moss and other lichen that ran in rivulets and larger patches of green and brown-yellow along its surface. It had been many years, since he was a young boy, that he last ventured into this area of the woods, along the deep outer regions of the town and of his home. He looked off to the east, to where the mining camp was and to where his home was and to where she still lay in their bed.

He walked the horse over to the well and looked deep within the darkness of the hole and he wondered silently who had built it. Who were its craftsmen, its architects? A frayed rope stretched downward into the abysmal black and he reached out slowly and took the rope. It was slick with some glossy grime that he could not decipher, and he pulled on the rope and felt the weight of the pail below being lifted. When the rusted can finally reached the top, he grabbed hold of it and looked inside at its contents. There was a black sludge that smelled of rotten fish, and on the top were the remains of what had once been a small bird, its bones and structure all that was left. The skull was turned upward, as if it were looking at the man, knowingly. The body of the bird seemed still intact, like if he had reached down and picked it up that the whole of the skeleton would lift and he would be able to throw it to the wind and watch it fly away from him.

He set the pail down on the ledge of the stone well and it was not until then that he realized the blur of the world from the tears he was crying, nor did he realize how much the wind had begun to blow. The trees above him were shaking, and leaves were falling down like an autumnal snowstorm. He raised his face to the sky and felt the warmth of the sun and he felt the tears of his face beginning to dry in the air and he heard the whispers within the wind. Truth and lies all the same.

The Rider knelt before the gray stone. Around him were scattered other small plots of ground similar to the one that lay before him, surrounding him. He reached his hand out and held it on the stone marker, as if draining from it some life force or maybe he was attempting to instill some unknown energy within the stone. Etched into the rock were words that he rubbed his hand gently over, trying to erase what they told him. Samantha MacAdams. In his head he counted the six year gap that she was alive.

His eyes closed then and he breathed deeply and thought of the passionate life that the girl could have lived, of the happiness and pain, the sorrow and the triumph, all one, all the same. He thought of her, of her marriage and love and children. They were all things lost forever in the numbers engraved in the stone; they were all things taken from this child. The Rider shook his head as he opened his eyes and looked again at the name; he pictured once more the image of the girl who lay beneath him, the girl held captive in the dust. And he realized that in the stone's markings that that name could not be undone, that it could not be erased or ever made right again.

Above him, in the upper sanctuary of the cemetery's chapel, there sounded the heavy toll of the church bell. He stood and looked behind him to where the black horse paced quickly back and forth, its head jerking violently, as if telling The Rider that someone was coming and that he needed to hurry. The Rider walked out of the small cemetery and mounted the horse and began to ride through the streets. As he approached the edge of the small town he looked back once more, a memory of the girl he never would know. The main thoroughfare of the town was busily filling with people: men, women, and children. All were dressed in their Sunday best.

Josiah rode slowly to the edge of the town and sat there for several minutes. They had come in through the blanketed trees of the woods that surrounded the small place. The horse was breathing heavily, and Josiah patted the side of the animal gently before urging it on with a quiet clicking of his tongue.

Just as he was entering the town, Josiah heard the steady toll of a bell. It sounded dull in the cool wind. He continued on, and, after a short while, Josiah saw the tall spire of the church from which the sound had come from. The spire rose high into the graying morning, and Josiah made his way toward it.

The town was small, with only a few square buildings, a combination of black wood and dirty brick fronts. The streets were clean, though, and he noticed this as he walked the horse into the far edge of the town. The white church stood on the opposite side of the town from where he was, but even so, the distance was no more than two hundred yards. Josiah's stomach tightened up and he felt thirsty. He dismounted from the horse and led the animal along the main road, deeper into the town. Several people, mostly women and children—and some men, also—were crossing the thoroughfare in front of him. They were each dressed elaborately—the men in full coats and black hats and the women in long dresses, some with small baskets that held what looked to be loaves of bread. The children were also dressed formally, with small dresses of blue and white for the girls and short vests and dark pants for the boys. These people all hurried in unison toward the church, and the boy followed after them, pulling the horse forward, his steps slowed by the heaviness of his mud-caked boots.

Near the entrance to the church, the boy tethered the horse to a post with a trough of water sitting before it. He entered the small, white building and took off his hat and sat in the rear pew of the church. The rest of the congregation was crowded as close to the front as possible and he noticed how the men and women were segregated from one another; he thought this strange. Josiah looked around the dusty church, feeling the damp warmth of the air on his skin. He took off his coat and set it on the wood pew next to him and faced forward.

After several minutes, a young man with slicked back hair, wearing a black shirt and black pants, stood from the front pew. He walked up the short steps and stood before the congregation. This man's arms were stretched wide, as if he were imitating Christ's stance on the cross. The whispers that had, until then, echoed within the small church stopped and Josiah could see the heads of each member bow down together. Josiah did not bow his head down, but left it up while he listened to the opening prayer of thanks from the minister. After the *Amen*, Josiah watched as the heads of the people around him slowly lifted.

He looked down at his blistered and cracked hands, dirty and brown. The lines stretching his palms stood out even more than normal and he traced these lines with his fingers until the minister began his sermon. Josiah returned his attention to the man standing alone before the group.

"Doctor Lansing has brought some terrible news to me early this morning. As you may have noticed, he, nor William and Maria Corvin join us this morning." A quiet monotone whisper seemed to escape from the congregation; men and women's heads turned slowly and bodies craned this way and that in hopes of confirming the minister's latest assertion. The minister continued: "The doctor is attending to Mrs. Corvin, who it seems was the victim of a robbery yesterday sometime at the Corvin house. She was injured, but the doctor has assured me that she will survive with little harm to her body. We can only thank our savior for this blessing. And, thus, we begin this morning's sermon with a word of prayer to God on her and William Corvin's behalf. If you would please bow your heads once more with me and give your most sympathetic prayers to them . . ."

After several seconds of silence the congregation raised their heads again and, as before, waited for the man standing before them to speak. The minister walked slowly across the small pulpit area and then returned to where he had been standing. In his hand was a small black Bible. Josiah looked at it and thought of his father. The minister took a deep breath and then continued the sermon.

"Little time has past since we lost our dear Samantha MacAdams. And now this event this morning . . ." His voice trailed off before he began again. "These events, though separate, are not very different from each other. Both of these events ask us to give pause and reflect on the frantic hustle of our lives. These events ask us to forget, even if so very briefly, the crops of our farms, the animals that we tend to, the minerals that we mine. We are asked to forget these things and consider ourselves as humans in God's kingdom." The minister's voice was quiet, deliberate and emotionless. "Take a look around you, right now. Go ahead. Look at the person next to you, behind you, across the row from you. Look at them. Look into their eyes, and try to see their souls."

The people in the rows turned awkwardly to look at one another. Josiah remained motionless, his eyes fixed on the minister, and no one turned to look at him.

"What do you see?" the minister asked.

No one answered. Silence seemed to settle completely in the small room. Not even the children seemed to move.

"Nothing? . . . I will tell you what I see. I'll tell you what I see when I look at you, or any man or woman or child's face for that matter. It is the same thing that I see when I look at the animals that surround us in the hills and woods. I see animals when I look at you all.

"Let me tell you this: if you truly study our world, as I have tried during my short time on this earth, you come to realize certain things about it and about us as this world's inhabitants.

"There is a barbarism to this place reminiscent of those early, holy times before Christ and his disciples. We have returned ourselves to those Old Testament times where blood runs through the streets and man is left to struggle alone and in fear. And whose doing is this?" The minister's voice had begun to rise slowly, almost imperceptibly, but it now dropped off again quickly, and he quietly whispered his answer:

"It has been our own doing. It has been yours and mine, everyone's doing. No one and no one thing other. The atrocities of this world, of what happened to Maria Corvin and the innocent Samantha MacAdams, of the violence and hatred that runs forth from our bodies and our animal desires, these atrocities need no God or devil, but simply man alone is enough. Beasts are what we have become. Beasts!" he called out. Then condemningly he whispered: "And we all have been charged with this crime against our creator."

Josiah looked at the members of the congregation. Some of the women had taken to fanning themselves and some of the men were scratching or shaking their heads slowly back and forth.

The minister paused and looked at the members; there was accusation in his eyes and he seemed to scowl at every one of the members before him. He took a drink of water and set the glass down. He continued: "In God's eyes, there is no delineation between sinners and sins. He abhors each equally. And this means that he abhors you all." The minister's voice became stronger and louder again. "We may blame Maria Corvin's troubles on vandals and thieves, but we are those vandals, we are those thieves. If we were to leave our safe haven of a town and we were to go and look at the collective troubles of every person on this earth, we will come to realize that it is not God's doing—it is man's. It is what man took from God and what man destroyed. There is no explanation for it. There is only truth that we are left with. Truth." He said it again, feeling the sour sound of the word in his mouth, spitting it out. "Truth. Sure and steady truth that does not waver, that does not bend, that does not lie." The man shook his head. He took several deep breaths before raising his voice even louder, now almost to a yell in the small church.

"God cast us from the garden and we are never to be allowed back in. And it is not his doing. But it is yours and it is mine. We are all entrenched in our own spite, discarded by our shared and individual wrath and our sinful reproaches, and we have been strewn down by the heavenly host of hosts by our own diseased hands. His son's death has occurred in vain, for man's sinful ways has spit on God's gift to him. Repentance is the only key we are allowed to still hold. And the road of awakening and the understanding of our emancipated hope is left in our own hands, for it has become our choice alone to look at our own reflections as individuals, as a collective group of people, as followers of a still loving God, and it is our choice to decide what we are to do with what we have been given." The minister was out of breath and he stopped and took another drink. The glass sounded throughout the small building when he set it back down.

He continued, his voice now calm, just above a whisper. All the men and women of the congregation leaned slightly forward in their seats, awaiting the minister's message, trying to hear the man more clearly. "Before man, there was Eden. Before man, there was still the wild of this place and in all places. And before man there was no pain and there was no punishment. But man has come and taken from this earth and taken from our gift and we are now left to walk within that valley of the shadow of death. And it is not until we can realize our diseased beings and give in fully to the repentance that God allows for us that we can possibly step into the light and feel the warmth of his love on our face. It is within you to decide your own fate, but remember that you do not act simply for you, but you act as a representative of all men and women and children who have come before you and who will come after you. It is your choice alone. And I can only say Amen to that."

The church went quiet as the minister finished. Each congregant remained in his or her seat, quietly staring at the floor. Some women were wiping tears from their faces, others were holding their children tightly.

The boy looked at his hands again and felt the rugged and worn leather skin and he quietly stood and left the church.

No one heard him stand and no one noticed him leave.

William Corvin

There's not much to talk about what happened between the time I set out on that train that mornin and when I come across her. In truth, it was a time I wish to forget. But time can't be forgotten. That's the thing bout it. It stays with you to the end, and eventually it's time that takes us all. I still can remember, as hard as I might try to not, the boys I joined with and things I've done and the things they've done. I stayed with them for near six years, and I wish to God every day that I had not. We started off sayin we'd only take what we needed. And we set out to the west, thinkin we could make it to the Pacific waters. One of us had heard of a city of gold in Mexico, and so we thought we might head there and search it out. But things fell out quick enough and I became a different person than ever I thought I could. I wanted to live some kind of adventure, that's what I told myself when I left, but I never thought that that adventure would take away my soul. There are many days still that I truly wonder if I still have a soul left. I reckon I do, but I reckon it's turned a soot black also, and it's a blackness that I cannot become clean of. In truth, I am afraid of that day when I stand before him for my judgment. I try to forget it and I hope that maybe he can too. But I don't reckon he can and I don't reckon I can either.

8

High in one of the dead branches of a tree above, a spider web glistened in the mid afternoon light. A small fly was caught in the sticky web. It flapped its wings hard and tried to wriggle its body free of the trap, but it could not. On the edge of the web was the spider, a black thing with hairy legs that gently stepped over the various strings it had made the previous day. Delicate and untouched. It walked slowly toward its prey but it stopped and hunched itself down closer to the soft web when the loud sound of two horses raced over the earth below. The sound lessened as the horses slowed and finally stopped just beneath the web and the spider.

The two men climbed off the unfamiliar horses and then walked a little distance from the animals to a small clearing area and sat on the moist ground that soaked through their pants and their coats, and they felt the cold on their bare legs. From the satchel, Wilkins brought out some bread that he had taken from the house and he broke it in two and handed the larger piece to the other man. They ate without talking, their mouths loudly chewing on the food. Cooper stood and walked over to the horses and took a small canteen of water from the saddle bag. He took a drink and then walked over to Wilkins and passed the canteen over to him and sat back down. He asked Wilkins what had happened in the house, but Wilkins only looked off to the direction they had come from and shook his head and continued to eat the bread.

When they finished the meal, they each took another drink of the water and then Wilkins took the bag and undid the strings and began to unload the bounty that he had taken from the house.

He laid the strange collection of items out in front of him and the other man moved closer towards the objects that rested on the ground. He picked some of the things up and looked at them closely, noticing the randomness of the collection, even now: silverware, some bronze candle holders, other metallic pieces.

"Ain't nothin here gonna make us a whole lot, Wilkins," Cooper said.

Wilkins reached deeper into the bag and pulled out some coins and laid them next to the forks and spoons and candlesticks.

"I couldn't stay long. Someone was up there, upstairs. She was comin down." He shook his head slowly. A few tears began to form and fall down his cheeks and he quickly wiped them away and looked off into the thick trees. He could still imagine her fallen body. His chest began to hurt.

Cooper nodded and then picked through the coins. He nodded his head again.

Wilkins turned his head back to the other. He snuffled loudly and then spat a yellow wad into the dirt next to him.

"You make it upstairs to the bedroom?" Cooper asked. His voice was calm. He looked at Wilkins and saw that there was a distance to the other's eyes.

Wilkins shook his head. "I was goin there, but I heard her comin down an I stopped an run out to you. Wasn't nothin to take, though. Wasn't nothin. I swear."

Cooper put his hand on Wilkins's leg gently. "That's fine. We'll find somethin else some other place, I reckon. At least you took some bread. My stomach been punchin itself out for a long while. Next town over we'll try to sell some these things. Might fetch us some coins yet."

Wilkins put the money in his coat pocket, and they began to carefully load the bag back up with the different items. They had almost finished when they heard the sharp and scuffled sound of leaves and twigs snapping from behind where they each sat, and they quickly looked at each other and then to where the sound came from. They could see nothing through the dark shadowed covering from the trees and the scattered bushes that lay here and there liked a fortress that held them without.

Wilkins reached to his side and drew his gun and pointed it toward the sound. Cooper had left his gun at the horse and stood quickly and ran to the horse but stopped and turned back when he heard the sound of three or four gunshots echo off the surrounds of this small place. Wilkins fired another two shots into the trees, his voice screaming out louder with each shot. Cooper turned back to the where the horses had been resting but they were gone now, fled from the sounds of the gunshots and into the shelter of the trees.

Cooper turned just as two other shots sounded in the small area and he saw Wilkins fall slowly to the ground, almost as if the man fell in a dream and Cooper could stop time completely if he so wanted. Cooper fell to his knees and watched as Wilkins lay on his side, the man's feet kicking back and forth and scraping into the earth, making small hills and rivets in the soil. Wilkins still held his gun and was firing it randomly into the wooded area around him until the gunshots stopped and all that was left was the dull sound of the empty chamber being turned over and again, clicking with each rotation. And still Wilkins continued to pull the trigger of the empty gun, screaming louder and louder with each imagined shot, unheard or seen.

Cooper called out from where he knelt, but his voice was cut short as another gunshot sounded and Wilkins's body jarred once more in a quick spasm and then lay completely still; the gun dropped from his grip and blood began to spill out from his head where this last bullet had struck him.

Cooper felt his chest tighten and his legs began to ache. He remained still, unable to flee, to follow the horses' tracks into the woods and find the gun that was stuck in the saddle. He raised his arms high above him, his body convulsing in short spasms. Spit began to collect at the edges of his mouth and fell in long prisms to the ground. "I give up," he called out.

From the shaded woods, a black horse walked slowly. It

seemed to be emerging from some nightmare that Cooper was a part of and Cooper bit his lip hard in hopes that he would wake. The rider of this horse was dressed in black and seemed to tower over everything in the small clearing from his height on the horse. This man held up a gun, pointing it directly at Cooper. Without lowering the gun's aim, The Rider dismounted and walked toward the kneeling man. As he approached closer, The Rider lowered his outstretched arm to his side. He stopped several steps in front of Cooper and stood quietly.

A cool breeze blew through the clearing and the leaves that were on the ground stirred and moved about and then rested still again. Tears were in Cooper's eyes and were running down his face, down his cheeks and off his nose, adding extra moisture to the ground below, where he knelt.

"Why'd you fire on me?" The Rider asked. His voice sounded calm.

Cooper shook his head. "I didn't. I didn't do nothin. He did." He motioned with his up-held arms. Through Cooper's tears he could see The Rider's face. A long scar stretched down the left side of it and seemed to burn.

The Rider turned and looked at the body behind him and then back to Cooper. "He your friend?"

Cooper stuttered, trying to find the right words. Finally, he said: "I knew him's all. We ain't no real friends."

The Rider laughed under his breath quietly and then nodded. "What's your name?" he asked.

"Mine?"

The Rider nodded. He kicked a leaf with his foot and looked back to the man kneeling.

"Robert Cooper." He spoke unsteadily, his voice low and cracking.

"Cooper." The Rider repeated the name out loud, as if trying to make it sound or feel right, or at least better on his own tongue. He looked at the sky and then back to Cooper. "All right, then. Stand up."

The other man did as The Rider told him.

"Over to your friend there." The two walked over to where Wilkins's body was. "Take a seat next to him. There you go, now."

Cooper did so. He quickly glanced over at Wilkins's face and saw the large oval carved into the dead man's cheek. It was a crater that was circled in a black rim with blood already beginning to dry around its edges. Pink stringy pieces seemed to hang all about the oval and spill out onto the ground. Cooper turned back to The Rider and saw that he had put his gun away and had now taken out a large knife and was wiping the blade of it on his pant's leg.

The Rider looked at Cooper. "Certain things you come to realize, Cooper. Certain universal truths, I suppose you can call it. One of them is the fact that if someone fires on you when you ain't doin nothin but tryin to seek out some food and drink, then that person or persons that fired ain't no friend. You agree, Cooper."

Cooper nodded. His lips began to tremble and he began to make small whimpering sounds. "We didn't mean nothing. He did it." Cooper began to whimper again, short gasping sounds.

The Rider knelt to where Cooper was and then suddenly raised the blade of the knife to Cooper's face and drew it quickly over the skin, cutting a short streak over the man's right cheek. Cooper screamed out in pain, short and loud, and fell back from The Rider.

The Rider lifted the blade and pointed the tip of it at Cooper's face. "Don't be doin none of that cryin in front of me. I seen women and children more strong and brave than you. Ain't no man can call himself such that cries like a baby."

Cooper held his hand to his face and nodded. Blood was spilling through his fingers. It felt warm on Cooper's hand.

The Rider continued: "Other truth you find is that someone don't shoot unprovoked. A person must be hidin or protectin somethin to shoot at someone else." He nodded and stood, looming tall over Cooper, who was cowering even lower to the ground now. "So, what you hidin?" The Rider turned and was searching the area with his eyes.

"Ain't hidin nothin. I swear to God."

The Rider turned back to Cooper. Surprise seemed to flood over his face and he knelt back down. "You swear to your heavenly maker? Odd choice of words for someone like you to tell me." He smiled. "Don't you swear nothin at me. You hear that clear?"

Cooper nodded. His breath was catching in his throat and his chest and his face continued to burn from the cut.

"And another thing," The Rider said, "Don't lie to me. I am your final judgment here. I am your final chance for salvation." He took the blade and plunged it deep into Cooper's thigh and kept it there.

Cooper cried out again, this time louder and longer.

"What you done?" The Rider demanded. He began to turn the blade with his hand, digging it deeper. "What you done?"

"We . . . we stole them things in that bag there. That's all."

The Rider removed the blade and wiped the blood on Cooper's shirt. "Stealin, huh? Ain't as bad as killin someone, is it?"

Cooper shook his head frantically. The Rider stood and walked over to the bag and opened it and emptied its contents onto the ground. The items clattered and spread out before him. Cooper began to crawl away, dragging his left leg behind him. Streaks formed in the soft ground from his boot. The Rider stood and watched Cooper moving away. "But, Cooper. God did tell Moses on top of the mountain that stealin is indeed just as bad as murder, and fornicatin, and covetin, and believin in false idols. Didn't he?"

Cooper continued crawling. His heart beat hard and he felt out of breath and wanted to stop and cry, but he continued moving away from The Rider. His arms and legs shook as he went and his face felt as if it were throbbing, expanding in and then outward.

"And here you are, Cooper. Here you are, stealin and worshipin this treasure here as your own idol, your own personal salvation. Only that ain't the real truth in life. That ain't no truth to be livin by at all. It's all sin. And we are told that the only payment for the wages of sin is death. And I am here to collect that payment."

He looked to the sky and to the treetops above him. He shook his head slightly. "Even though I wish it weren't me."

The Rider looked down at his hands. For a moment he thought he saw red streaks spread across his palms and he wiped them on his pant's legs and then looked again. They were clean of any marks. He did not know why, but he felt tears starting to well up in his eyes. He looked up at Cooper again and felt a certain remorse for the man, or it could have been envy, he was not sure.

After several seconds, The Rider walked over to where Cooper crawled and looked down at the man. Cooper dug his hands into the soft mud, still trying to leave the clearing, as if his salvation awaited him in the cover and protection of the trees. "Ask for your forgiveness. Cooper?"

Cooper stopped his struggle and looked up at The Rider. His face was covered in mud and dirt and filth and he looked up with red eyes from the tears that he had spilled. Blood ran down his face and mixed in with the grime from the ground and spit and mucous clung and bubbled from his mouth and nose.

"Ask for forgiveness. Ask for it." The Rider's voice sounded now as a whisper. "Please."

Cooper softly said he was sorry and he turned quickly to the woods that were just out of his reach and then he looked back at The Rider.

The Rider nodded, and the tears began to fall freely from his eyes so that he could hardly see the man in front of him or see what his own hands were doing, and the whole time he was telling himself in his mind to stop and leave, but he couldn't stop. He couldn't.

And high in the tree above these men, the fly no longer moved. The spider had wrapped the prey in its webbing completely and was beginning to eat the body of the insect in some primal eucharist of life and survival and of death.

They stopped next to the running stream. Josiah left the horse behind him near the water, not bothering to tether the animal to a tree, and went off and collected berries from the still cold plants that were spread on the ground like a colorful blanket of reds and blues and purples; some of the berries still had frost from the night before and had turned a white-gray shade and he didn't pick these. He sat next to the small stream and ate them. They tasted bitter and made his saliva build up and collect under his tongue and he swallowed the saliva and it tasted sweet and warm. The horse lapped from the stream and before long the boy joined him.

Josiah looked at the horse and then felt the skin of his own belly. They had grown thin and gaunt these two haggard beings, the boy and the horse. He rubbed his hands over his cold and wet face and felt the small hairs on his cheeks and his chin. He stood and began to walk along the muddy bank of the stream, walking in the opposite direction of the water's flow; he noticed the melting ice coverings along the outer regions of the water's reach where the shade from above still covered the stream.

After some time of pushing his way through the dense groupings of bushes, he came across a large rock that seemed out of place in this thickly forested part of the woods. Josiah circled the rock, slowly dragging his fingers along the rough surface of the granite, and he imagined how such a monstrous thing could simply exist without any reason or seeming history. He looked around the area and could see no brother or sister of this rock. It was alone, as was he. Josiah had almost circled the rock in full when he noticed the white and red lines along the surface, covering the fissures and crevices, hiding the imperfections, and he began to clear away the rusted dirt and moss, scraping it away with his dirty fingernails, until he saw the ancient figures beneath. They were hieroglyphs upon the rock's skin that had been drawn there by an artist who would forever remain unknown. He studied them. On the left side was a red beast reared up on two back legs, its forefeet raised upward towards a red sun or moon—he could not tell which—and before this beast were three figures drawn in a ghostly white and they seemed to be brandishing weapons—spears or daggers or swords—or maybe they were simply offering tithing gifts to this beast. The boy placed his hand on the boulder, covering these paintings, hoping to erase these memories that were not his own to erase. The rock felt warm from the sun.

After several minutes, Josiah returned to the stream, back to where the horse grazed and walked uncertainly along the wet ground. The boy looked up and down the stream and decided that he would eventually follow in the direction that the water moved. He hoped that the south had something to offer him that he could not find in the northern parts of this land. But his legs felt tired and worn and his body heavy, and he decided to close his eyes and rest for some time before moving on.

He sat against one of the trees near where the horse was and he fell asleep to the sound of the water passing over the smooth rocks and of the animal eating what grass there remained along the shores of the stream; though in his dreams he could hear nothing.

William Corvin

I had set off from the rest of them a few months before and was wanderin the land in search of somethin. What it was, I still don't reckon I know. I don't suppose I was meant to know even. When I left them we had begun to move south and were in the northern regions of Texas . . . I left them all after I shot that young kid. That's what did it. I still see his face, no expression every time I see it. He was maybe twenty—not much younger than I was then—and I'd taken what little he had on him. The rest of them had all taken to the other men that that boy was travelin with and they stripped that coach bare and the bodies of the men they killed. We had hidden ourselves up behind some trees on a small hill, havin tracked that coach for miles. When they were below us, we came chargin down the hill on foot and we were all shootin wild. That boy was the only one not in the coach—he was ridin himself on a neat brown horse and I was the first one to be runnin. I can remember as I lifted the gun that he didn't even reach for his gun but just looked at me and waited, like he knew what was happenin and he wasn't about to try to counter the inevitable. Guess he figured it's just fate, and I don't have much reason to argue with him there. But anyways, after I fired and I watched him fall from that horse and watched that horse gallop away, I searched him and found in his pocket a thin piece of iron metal, and I took that and I took the few coins that he had and I put them in my pocket without lookin at any of it. I left him facedown next to grouping of skinny cedars that we'd hid behind.

I imagine there wasn't much of his face left and I didn't want to look, so I left him where he fell and that was about all with him. I looked down at him as I ran away and realized just what I'd done and that's when I decided to leave them. I ran off and didn't look back and didn't tell them I was goin. After walkin for damn near a day and a half by myself I decided to stop in one of the small towns I was passin through and it wasn't til I went into that room that I looked at that iron thing I'd took. The image on it's scratched face was nearly worn off and it left only a light outline of her. She was a young and pretty girl standin in a long white dress in the middle of a great big room. And I remember thinkin even then that her eyes seemed so soft and so carin and full of life, and I imagined her waitin for this boy to come back to her and how he would never do so and I began to weep and I fell to the ground and buried my head into my hands. I remember lookin at my reflection in the mirror there and seein my red eyes and the dirt on my face and on my hands. I did not recognize the face and I did not know what to do. And I drew from my belt my gun and pulled the hammer back and stuck the cold barrel beneath my jaw. My hand was shakin and spit was streamin from my mouth and my nose and tears fell down from my eyes and then I heard the door open and shut, and I saw her. She was just some skinny, pretty dark skinned girl from some place I had never been—Mexico, Spain maybe. It never really mattered to me. And it seemed like an instant after I saw her come in to that room that she had taken the gun from me, snatchin it from my hands and placin it on the bed away from where I was. And she kneeled down on the ground beside me and put her hands on mine and told me things were all right. And I believed her. She had tears in her eyes too and I asked her her name and she told me that it was Maria and she asked me if I still wanted her to stay and I nodded and she lay with me all night, her hand over my chest and her breath on my neck. The next day I put the metal photo in my pocket and left the money for her and then left the place, but I had only gone a mile or so out of the town when I thought back on the girl and I turned the horse around and went back and talked to the man there and asked him how much he would take for her and he told me and I gave him all that I had saved from the years I had been away and we left the hotel and the town together, both ridin the same horse, and we returned home. When we got there, I found an empty lot of land, grass burned from the summer sun and no one save Jefferson, him still tendin to what animals and plants survived. The vegetable crops were nearly dead, every last one: what corn we had had fallen from the stocks to the ground and been chewed and picked at by birds and squirrels and deer, and what was left on the pieces were burnt black, parts that not even the animals would eat. And off in the distance, Jefferson told me, the mines were cleared out and he would go down there every few days with a shotgun and run off any squatter or such person that tried to mine the coal by their own two hands and sell it themself. 'Is your land, Mr. Corvin,' he told me, 'And I aim to keep it that way such you should finally come home as you done.' I asked why he hadn't left like the rest and he looked at me and told me that his wife and two daughters were there still and that there was nowhere else he would go to. 'They stayed,' he said, 'And so will I' . . . The following month I married Maria in the church up in the town there. I asked Jefferson to stand next to me during the ceremony, and he did.

9

A breeze has now just started and it sweeps across the dry and brittle grassland. It creates an ocean's wave that bends and twists the grass in time to the ancient melody of the air so that as one section ceases to move forward or to the other side the next section after begins its own movement in a continuation. And this happens, with each ripple casting itself further off along the grassfield, and you would think that if given chance this wave of the land would continue on to the edges of this world and possibly beyond, if only there were.

William Corvin rested his horse in the middle of the marked road. He knew that the men would not take to the road, but he continued along it regardless. He climbed off the horse and stood on the ground and brushed the hair along the horse's face. Corvin walked several steps further up the road before he stopped and turned back to the horse. He knelt and closed his eyes. In his mind he could see the men he pursued, could see them riding the horses they had taken from the barn. He could see these men's faces, and he imagined riding up behind them and pulling his pistol from his belt and firing at each man, and he imagined them falling from the horses and how he would stand over their bodies and how each man would beg him for mercy but he would only raise the gun again and shoot each man in the head. Corvin imagined how the blood would spray quickly across the ground and then the slow trickle of it as it escaped each man's head. And he would walk away and get back on his horse and ride and the bodies of these men would be picked at by the animals of the woods.

And then Corvin opened his eyes and looked up the road and then back at his hands. From his back pocket he pulled the thin metal tintype out and looked at the picture of the girl. As he had so many other times before this, he studied her features, tracing her outline with his finger, and he thought of this girl and then of Maria. He imagined Maria as the picture on the iron and how she would be without him and him without her. He stood and walked to the roadside and knelt again and dug a small hole in the loose ground and then laid the photo in the hole and covered it up again with the earth, and he stood and walked back to his horse and climbed back on and turned it to where he had come from.

Behind him the road stretched. It was a road that would carry him to some distant town with a fixed distance, and maybe he would come across these men, or maybe he wouldn't. But the road continued on regardless, and he would not take this road. Instead, he would travel a different one, an empty road that could not be measured in miles or feet, but one only distanced by time and event, by the past and what the future might contain. He rode now back to Maria, he rode now back home, and he could think of nothing else but holding her in his arms and telling her that things would be all right.

The camp was only a few yards from the shores of the river. He turned slowly when he came to it and he felt his stomach tighten and his throat close. The Rider stopped the horse and slowly climbed from the beast and walked among the scene.

Surrounding the perimeter of this vacant place were seven different tents, all made of different material, and these tents whipped about in the wind and sounded of ripping burlap or of a woman swatting heavy sheets with a broom after laundry. But he could not hear this sound, nor could he hear the river flowing behind him, nor the sounds of birds high in the branches above him, nor his own heavy feet or his breath as he walked the grounds. He was barely aware of his shaking hands. His stomach felt hard and he tasted bile in his throat and he bent over, trying to rid himself of this but he could not. He could only cough and spit up saliva. He knelt down and placed his forehead on the dirt and let his tears grow and then they fell directly into the earth's ground. In his head he whispered the words over and over again. "My God. My God."

Just before where he knelt, in the center of the camp area, was a large fire pit, its ashes long since cooled, and surrounding this pit, spaced evenly apart, were the heads of twelve or thirteen people, men and women, and they were all placed on sharp poles of metal dug deep into the ground—a grotesque and monstrous picket fence. The dry and swollen bodies of these scarecrows were strewn around the camp haphazardly; the rotting bodies laying where they fell.

Next to The Rider was a small doll that a baby might play with, and when he lifted his head, he frantically looked around the area for an infant to who this doll belonged, but he could find none. He took up the doll and looked into the button eyes and felt the soft pillow tenderness of the thing and he brought it to his face and wept into it, asking himself over and over what his place was in a world that had spun so far out of his own control, asking himself whether he or any other person or demigod of the earth could offer true redemption or salvation to the people of this pagan land. And he called out in a scream of primal terror and pain and confusion. Above him the birds flew from their tendril perches, some still with pieces of flesh in their beaks.

Josiah heard the scream, and it sounded clearly to him, as if the wind had carried it from its source directly to where he now was. His stomach felt in knots and the cry sounded of an animal, something strange and cruel, something truly pained. His mouth began to satiate with the thought of meat and his head began to ache; he dug his heels into the sides of the horse and the two began to move at a quicker pace. The stream that he had been following down had been joined by several other streams over the course of his journey and it had since turned into a river. He followed it along still, hoping that the water would lead him to the animal's sound.

After some time, the boy could see smoke rising above the trees—black and thick. He eventually came upon the clearing. The first thing he saw was the source of the smoke: a blackened pit stretching across the wet and muddy ground some ten feet in diameter. The flames were violent and bright and he could feel the whisperings of the heat even from where he was.

Josiah looked beyond the pit and saw the tents—thin paper coverings flapping loosely in the wind. He led the horse slowly into the camp; the closer he came to the pit, however, the more he noticed the putrid air. He began to gag on the sickly sweet smell of rot. He climbed from the horse, his gun clasped tightly in his hands, and began to walk into the heart of the camp. Within the orange and red blaze of the pit he saw the bodies. They were heaped upon one another and he had to turn his face from the blaze, not from the morbid sight of the skin turning black and falling off the bones or the clothing burning a bright yellow but because of the heat from the flames. When he turned, he noticed just how close the camp was to the river and then he saw the man.

And it needed no announcement, no expectation, no hint even. The boy simply looked upon the man dressed in black. The man whose face was unshaven. The man who wore a slash along the left side of his face that shined brightly in the sun. The man who was standing in the middle of the water:

He is without a coat and his sleeves are pushed up to his shoulders so that the fabric makes his arms look three times the size they really are, as if he wears padding on his shoulders like some ancient soldier. In his right hand is a knife and running the lengths of his arms are thin streaks of blood that seem to coat his flesh in a new and alien layer of skin. This man is crying and he continues to slash at his arms, but the tears do not seem to come because of the cuts that he is making, but they instead come from some other, deeper pain.

The Rider felt the ice cold water surrounding his legs. He walked stagnantly out into the river, not realizing where he was or what he was doing. After several minutes of standing in the water, his legs went numb and he could not feel the cold anymore. He took off his jacket and let it fall in the water; the steady current grabbed hold of it and took it downriver so that he could no longer have seen it if he chose to look, but he did not. Instead, The Rider took the sleeves of his shirt and pushed them up to his shoulders and then pulled from his belt the knife that had struck down so many before him. He looked at the blade and felt his stomach turn. His fingertips began to tingle as if he had electricity running through his veins. His hands felt warm.

He slowly dug the blade into the skin of his left arm and pulled down. The blade separated the flesh easily and he felt his arms begin to burn. He made a six inch slit and then raised the blade back up on his arm and began another cut. His dried eyes began to tear again as he made more cuts, the blade becoming quicker and more sure with the more cuts he made. His arms had ceased to pain, showing now the counterfeit stigmata. His skin now had a dull, anxious feeling, as if eagerly awaiting the next cut that would come. Blood was streaming down his arm to his fingertips and it felt sticky and cool on his hands.

After uncountable cuts to his left arm, The Rider moved the blade to his left hand, almost dropping the blade in the river water as he transferred it. He managed, though, to hold onto the handle and began to make slow cuts along his right arm. These cuts were more jagged than the others had been and hurt him much more than the ones on his left arm. He began to sob and was just about to drop the blade and fall to his knees in the water when he looked up and saw the boy standing in front of him. This boy held a rifle in his hand, but it was pointed down at the ground.

The boy called out to him, but The Rider could not hear the call. Instead, The Rider could only hear the steady thumping sound of his heartbeat in his temples. The boy looked over to where The Rider's horse stood in the water and then back to The

Rider and raised the rifle quickly. The lifted rifle shook violently before the boy steadied it, and The Rider dropped the blade into the water. Then he heard the sound of the gun fire.

It was not until he was laying in the water, feeling the cold current take him downstream, that The Rider felt the pain in his chest or realized where he now was. He raised his head enough to look at his feet, then the shore, the dogwood trees still in blossom, some of the white flowers still clinging to the branches while others had fallen into the water and, like him, were being carried away to some other place.

And before the world went black, The Rider thought he saw a man emerging from behind one of the trees along the shore of this river without a name. It was an old man whose head looked to be covered in a large black hat and whose face looked red and folded upon itself; The Rider thought he saw a crutch or a long, ocher blade in this man's hands, and he thought that he saw this man smile but he could not be sure of it, nor could he be certain that the man was even there. And then The Rider let the darkness consume him until he could not see anything but the dark and could not hear a sound, save for his own breath and the beating of his own heart now growing more and more faint.

It was not until the boy looked over and saw the black horse in the water up to its knees that the boy realized who stood before him. He called out to this man, but the man gave no recognition of hearing him. Josiah raised the gun slowly, leveling it at the man in the water, feeling the true weight of the thing. He could see a long, red mark running down the left side of this man's face and Josiah aimed for this mark. For a while—what in reality was merely seconds but to the boy seemed so much longer—Josiah stared down the barrel, trying to keep the gun steady, trying to slow his breathing, just as his father had taught him years before. Then he exhaled quietly and eased back the cold trigger of the gun. The piercing sound of the gun's fire erupted through the boy's world and he watched as The Rider fell into the water in a heavy splash. The blood and the water ran together around the man's body in swirling unison so that you could not tell one from the other.

The boy stood without moving on the shore of the river. He could not move. He had felt the heavy thrust of the gun under his shoulder, and he did not know what he was supposed to think, or what he was supposed to do now. Now that it was.

He tried to smile, but he could not. He could only watch the black horse run through the river, its feet violently splashing the water behind it and onto its back. And he watched as the horse reached the other side of the river and disappeared into the thicket of trees.

Then he turned and walked away from the river and from The Rider whose body was quietly being carried along the current.

Years later, on the night that he will die, after he has grown old and seen his children come and grow and his grandchildren after them, Josiah will look up to the darkness of the sky, where no star burns overhead and no moon sits above him to keep watch over him. He will remember this moment and the sound, the shattering sound of it, and it will seem as if his finger has just pulled the heavy trigger and his body has just braced for the shot and been rocked jarringly back by the force of it. On this distant night he will see again the man crumple and fall before his eyes, and he will watch as the water splashes and creates innumerable waves that stretch to some distant shore that he now, in his ancient age, sits on the bank of. And on this night he will become that boy again, still without any of the answers that he wishes to learn, without any of the feelings he desires so badly to understand. He will try to call back through the years to that boy, but his voice will go hoarse from calling and he will finally stop. And as an old man he will walk off again, but instead of the sun and the light there will only be dark and quiet and the thoughts of what will come to be yet, as it remains a ghost that forever haunts him.

Josiah Fuller

There's been many a night since that day that I have stopped and looked down at my hands an looked at em up close like there was some hidden power in em that I did not know or understand fore I pulled the trigger of that gun that day and shot him. When I look at my hands, I usually think of my mother and wonder what she would think of me and my ways and my life and how I am now and what I've become, but then I remember that she is dead, and in a way I feel that I am also. An when I look at my hands an I remember my mother an I think of my father an how he was always readin his Bible at night an I see em as I last saw em, hangin from that tree. An when that happens, I can only think to myself: who am I? Or, maybe worse yet, what am I? An I have looked at my reflection in the water an on a glass storefront an I can't help but wonder if that reflection is truly me or if it is someone else, some other mask that's there in place of who I am, an many a times I look away fast so as not to see what face it really is that looks back at me. Someday, though, I hope that I will be able to look at myself and feel right with what I done an who I am. But that time is not now, an I do not think that that time will ever truly come. Oh, how I wish it will, though. I think in my head softly, sayin it over and over to myself, 'Please come, Please come and let me forget.'

Epilogue

The small wooden structure that once ignited the sky, throwing out brilliant colors in the darkness, is now nothing but a blackened outline against the night. In its place, animals large and small now seek shelter there—a sanctuary from the cold winds and the harsh land. A refuge for the illwanted. In time it will grow more decrepit and more defunct so that one day it will disappear entirely, vanishing in the master illusionist's greatest act. And when this happens, after the buildings of men fall and the iron rusts, after the bodies of men and women return complete to the soil, the animals will once again be given dominion over the woods and forests and streams. And in the deep glens and the open clearings and fields of the world we will no longer exist as we are now but we will instead have become faded memories of some time from long ago that cannot be brought back again.

CPSIA information can be obtained at www.ICGtesting.com
Printed in the USA
LVOW09*1837071114

412566LV00002B/10/P